ALL NIGHT LONG

The waterlogged shack looked dark and creepy, not in the least bit romantic. Inside it was damp and chilly.

"I'm cold," Jessica said. "Let's go back to the beach."

"Don't worry," Scott promised huskily. "I'll warm you up."

Suddenly he was kissing her in a way that told her he meant business. Jessica backed away.

"Scott, I—" She held out an arm to ward him off, but he mistook it for an invitation.

He was all over her, tugging insistently at her bikini straps while he devoured her neck. The muscles she'd admired on the beach felt knotted and menacing now. His demanding lips pressed against hers. *No— not this way*, she thought. She'd always been able to control her boyfriends when she wanted to, but Scott was more of a man than a boy, she realized with rising panic. Someone who wasn't about to take no from a girl who had led him on.

Jessica sensed she was in deep trouble.

Bantam Books in the Sweet Valley High Series
Ask your bookseller for the books you have missed

SWEET VALLEY HIGH

ALL NIGHT LONG

Written by
Kate William

Created by
FRANCINE PASCAL

BANTAM BOOKS
TORONTO · NEW YORK · LONDON · SYDNEY · AUCKLAND

RL 6, IL age 12 and up

ALL NIGHT LONG
A Bantam Book / February 1984
11 printings through January 1987

Sweet Valley High is a trademark of Francine Pascal

Conceived by Francine Pascal

Produced by Cloverdale Press, Inc.

Cover art by James Mathewuse

ISBN 0-553-26742-6

Published simultaneously in the United States and Canada

Bantam Books are published by Bantam Books, Inc. Its trademark, consisting
of the words "Bantam Books" and the portrayal of a rooster, is Registered in
U.S. Patent and Trademark Office and in other countries. Marca Registrada.
Bantam Books, Inc., 666 Fifth Avenue, New York, New York 10103.

PRINTED IN THE UNITED STATES OF AMERICA

O   20   19   18   17   16   15   14   13   12

ALL NIGHT LONG

One

"What do you think? Do I look sophisticated enough for Scott?" Jessica Wakefield stood poised before the full-length mirror in her twin sister's bedroom, chin thrown back, her lovely features arranged in a languid pout.

Elizabeth glanced up from the note pad she was scribbling on. "Brooke Shields you're not. Besides, why do you care what Scott thinks?" Her eyes narrowed in suspicion. "You're *not* thinking of going to that party at the lake? Not after Mom—"

Jessica whirled on her twin, cutting her dead with a look of defiance. "Who says she has to know? You've heard the old saying—what you don't know won't hurt you."

1

Her eyes, which normally hovered somewhere between blue and green, and could go either way depending on her mood, glittered pure emerald fire.

"And just how do you plan on getting away with it? Mom's not exactly blind, you know." Elizabeth noticed the corners of Jessica's mouth turning up—the mouth that was a carbon copy of her own but capable of oh-so-much-more mischief. "Uh-oh. Forget I even asked. I don't think I want to know the answer. Just remember—whatever it is, don't include me."

Jessica's smile deepened into one of pure innocence. Her eyes looked blue now, as blue as a baby's. She went back to admiring her reflection, scooping her sun-streaked blond hair up on top of her head as she struck a new femme fatale pose.

"I haven't the vaguest idea what you're talking about," she drawled. "*I'm* spending the day with Cara."

Elizabeth rolled her eyes. "Since when does Cara have a mustache and drive a red Firebird? Come on, Jess, who do you think you're kidding? You can't keep a thing like this a secret. Besides, I think Mom's right. Scott *is* too old for you."

If first impressions counted for anything—and Elizabeth happened to think they did—then Scott's age wasn't the only black mark against him. She remembered the insolent way he'd looked her up and down when Jessica had introduced her to him the previous week. There had been a dumb, leering smile on his face when he'd made the old joke about them being "double the fun." Elizabeth had nearly gagged. When he peeled away from the curb in his tomato-red Firebird, he'd left a squiggly trail of skid marks in his wake. Elizabeth had thought college boys were supposed to be above that kind of thing, but apparently she was wrong.

And so was Jessica. But it wouldn't be the first time.

Elizabeth sighed. She was only four minutes older than her twin, but sometimes she felt it was more like four years. Jessica had a habit of attracting trouble the way a magnet attracts metal shavings. And more often than not, big sister Elizabeth was the one she turned to to bail her out when the water got a little too deep. The problem was that no matter how much Elizabeth protested, Jessica knew her sister would always end up helping her out. And she unhesitatingly took advantage of that whenever she thought she could.

Only this time it wouldn't work, Elizabeth told herself resolutely. For emphasis, she even wrote in black felt pen under the notes she'd been scribbling for her "Eyes and Ears" column, which appeared weekly in Sweet Valley High's newspaper, *The Oracle*: "May a band of wild

3

pygmies hang me by the thumbs if I let Jess get me involved in this."

She sighed again. Jessica had turned away from the mirror and was busy rummaging through Elizabeth's bureau drawers. The twins were the same size—a perfect six—and Elizabeth didn't really mind when Jessica borrowed her clothes. She just wished that, for once, she would get them back in the same condition in which they'd gone out. More often than not, she ended up having to fish them out from under Jessica's bed or from the crumpled heap at the back of her closet, which Jessica kiddingly referred to as the "compost pile."

"This halter top would look really sexy with my red shorts," Jessica said, holding up a scrap of lacy white cloth as she smiled sweetly at her twin. "You don't mind, do you, Lizzie?"

"I wouldn't want to look too sexy around Scott if I were you," Elizabeth warned darkly. "It might be like waving a red cape in front of a bull."

With a toss of her sun-streaked mane, Jessica flopped onto the bed beside her sister, scattering the articles Elizabeth had been proofreading for *The Oracle*.

"What's wrong with sex appeal?" she demanded, arching an eyebrow. "Actually, if you want to know the truth, you could use a little more of it yourself. Not that you're not gor-

4

geous." Jessica laughed and fluttered her eye-lashes at the sister who was her mirror image.

"Naturally." Elizabeth giggled.

"You just need to play it up more. You know, like in all those ads where the mousy secretary lets her hair down and undoes the top button of her blouse, and suddenly everyone in the office notices what a knockout she is."

With a dubious expression, Elizabeth fingered her ponytail. "If letting my hair down means attracting guys like Scott, forget it. I'd rather be mousy."

She'd been invited to the party at the lake along with Jessica, but Elizabeth had been re-lieved when their mother had vetoed the idea. Scott and his friends were all older than the kids they usually hung around with. Jessica said that Scott was eighteen, but Elizabeth suspected she'd conveniently shaved a year or two from his real age in order to convince their parents he wasn't too old for her.

Anyhow, it wasn't the age difference that bothered her so much as the reputation Scott's gang had. Elizabeth had heard stories about the wild parties held at some of the college dor-mitories. Her best friend Enid's older cousin had even been to one. It was a kind of grown-up pajama party, she'd reported, with everyone wearing nightshirts and nightgowns, and the floor strewn with mattresses for them to sit on instead of chairs. According to Enid's cousin, things had gotten pretty far out of hand, especially with all the drinking that was going on.

A beach party at the lake in the daytime sounded innocent by comparison, but with that crowd it seemed as if almost anything could happen, Elizabeth mused.

Jessica, however, wasn't going to let her sister's doubts ruin her good time. "OK by me if you want to sit around for the rest of your life," she snapped. "I'm not going to let it stop *me* from having fun. I'm sixteen, not sixty like *some* people I know," she added with a pointed look at her twin.

"Even if it means possibly getting caught and being grounded for the next five thousand years?" Elizabeth asked.

"What could go wrong? I've got the perfect alibi. Cara's family is driving up the coast for the day, and they invited me to go with them. It's all arranged. Ask Mom."

"She believed you?"

Jessica switched on her innocent smile once again. "Why shouldn't she? Is this the face of a liar?"

"Yes!" replied Elizabeth without hesitation.

"I didn't really lie." Jessica stuck out her lower lip in an exaggerated pout. "I just rearranged the truth a little. I told Mom Cara had *invited* me to go along. I didn't exactly say I was *going*."

6

Elizabeth snorted. "Save it for the judge at your trial. I've never heard anything so pathetic in my whole life."

Jessica was clearly annoyed. "You know something?" Her eyes flashed with scorn. "I think you're jealous."

"Jealous over Scott? You've got to be kidding! He's definitely not my type. Come to think of it, I don't think he's *your* type, either."

"And just what is that supposed to mean?"

"It means I think he's too old for you, for one thing."

"He's the same age as Steve," Jessica pointed out, referring to their brother.

"I don't think Steve would want a girl to sneak around behind her parents' back to go out with him."

"You don't even know Scott!"

"That's just the point. Neither do you. What if things get out of hand up at the lake? How will you get home? None of those kids are your friends."

"I can take care of myself," Jessica announced sullenly.

"The way you took care of yourself with Bruce?" Elizabeth reminded her.

Handsome, popular Bruce Patman. Jessica had really been hung up on him for a while. And he had used her without regard for anyone's feelings but his own. Fortunately, Jessica had gotten the last laugh. But Elizabeth wasn't sure she'd be so lucky with someone older and more experienced like Scott.

"Bruce has nothing to do with this. Besides," Jessica rationalized, "I never really liked him anyway."

Elizabeth knew differently, but she decided not to argue. She tried another tack. "What about the test, then? How do you expect to pass it when you've been out partying the whole day before?"

The test for the tourist guide license was scheduled for the day after the party. If the twins passed, they would be able to earn extra money over their summer vacation giving tours of Sweet Valley's beautiful coastline and its other scenic attractions. This was something both girls had been planning for a long time, and Elizabeth knew it wouldn't be nearly as much fun without Jessica.

"I'll take care of the test, if *you* promise not to tell Mom," Jessica bargained, shrewdly detecting a chink in Elizabeth's armor.

"I'm not promising anything. If she asks me, I'm not going to lie."

Jessica leaped from the bed, facing Elizabeth squarely, hands planted on her hips. "Some friend you are!"

Unfazed, Elizabeth replied dryly, "I'm probably the best friend you've got, Jess. You just don't know it."

Jessica cast her a withering look. "Don't do me any favors. Just don't come running to me someday if you ever need my help." Abruptly she burst into tears. "I thought sisters were supposed to stick up for each other," she choked.

Elizabeth caught her lower lip between her teeth. Maybe she had been too harsh. "Jess . . ."

But Jessica had already done an about-face. She strode out of the room, and Elizabeth flinched as the door slammed shut behind her.

"Why let it bug you?" questioned Enid Rollins, Elizabeth's closest friend. "You're not doing anything wrong."

It was Sunday, and they'd stopped at the Dairi Burger for a bite to eat on their way to the beach. Elizabeth had ordered her favorite, a hot dog dripping with chili, but she could only pick at it. Her mind was on Jessica roaring up to the lake in a red Firebird.

"I haven't done anything wrong *yet*," she amended. "I just hope my mom doesn't get suspicious and ask me for the truth."

"So? If she does, tell her." Enid fixed her big green eyes firmly on her friend.

There was no love lost between Enid and Jessica—not after the low-down, rotten trick Jessica had pulled that had just about cost Enid her reputation. Even though it had all worked out, Enid would never count Jessica as a friend. In her opinion, it would be like asking a boa constrictor to dinner.

Elizabeth sighed. "It's not that simple. She *is* my sister, after all. I wouldn't want to see her get into any trouble."

Enid couldn't help but wonder what Jessica would have done if their roles had been reversed. She refrained from saying anything; Elizabeth could be touchy on the subject of her twin.

"Look," said Enid, forking in a mouthful of coleslaw. "You're here to have fun—so have fun. Let Jessica worry about Jessica." She tossed her dark hair with finality.

The beach was fairly crowded by the time they arrived, shortly past noon. Elizabeth and Enid spread their towels near the lifeguard station, which would provide a few patches of shade from the scorching sun. A lean yet muscular boy with seal-brown hair materialized just as Elizabeth was unscrewing the cap from a tube of suntan lotion.

"Turn around and I'll get your back," he ordered, snatching the tube from her hands before she could protest.

"Todd!" she laughed, submitting to a vigorous rubdown at her boyfriend's enthusiastic hands. Her heart beat a little faster at his nearness.

Playfully he dabbed a spot of lotion on the end of her nose and rubbed it in gently, his brown eyes regarding her with unconcealed affection.

"Where's Jessica?" he asked.

"Uh . . ." For a moment Elizabeth was at a loss for words. She knew Todd disapproved when she covered up for her sister.

"Cara," Enid put in hastily. "She's with Cara." Mentally she shook her fist at Jessica for putting Elizabeth on the spot.

Elizabeth pretended a sudden fascination with the waves breaking offshore in perfect blue-green formation. Just beyond the surf line, an antlike cluster of wetsuited, black shapes was paddling into the next swell. As the wave crested, one of them broke away from the others, swooping ahead into the curl with the grace of a dolphin.

"He's good," Elizabeth remarked, shading her eyes. "Whoever he is."

"That's Sonny Callahan," Todd answered. "And you're right, he is good. He came in first at last year's state surfing championship. I hear he's competing this year, too."

"Does Bill know?" Enid asked.

To Bill Chase, surfing was practically more important than breathing. He'd gone all out to

11

train for the championship. The regionals were only a week away. Bill was good; they all knew that. But was he good enough to beat Sonny?

"What do *you* think?" They all followed Todd's gaze as he looked toward a lone towheaded figure perched on a rock at the end of the jetty, staring out to sea.

"Poor Bill," said Elizabeth. "He must really be depressed if he's not in the water on a day like this."

Actually, it was almost impossible to tell *what* Bill was thinking, most of the time. He stayed pretty much to himself, and at school he didn't belong to any particular group. Elizabeth thought he was probably just shy, but Jessica liked to believe he was some kind of mystery man. Elizabeth remembered the time her sister had invited him to a Sadie Hawkins dance, as if she were bestowing some great honor on him. When he turned her down, Jessica's rage had nearly blown the roof off. Someday she was going to turn the tables on him, she had sworn. Someday—

"Hey," Todd's voice interrupted Elizabeth's reverie. "Isn't that Cara?" They watched a pretty brunette in a pink bikini making her way down the beach. "I thought you said she was with Jessica."

Elizabeth's heart sank into her sandals. What was Cara doing *here*? Had Jessica invented the entire story about Cara's family driving up the coast?

Pretending she was going to get a drink of water, Elizabeth caught up with Cara and asked her what had happened. Cara explained that last-minute car trouble had forced her father to abandon their plans for the day.

"What about Jessica?" Elizabeth worried aloud. "What if she gets found out?"

"Jessica's a big girl." Cara peered at her through a pair of sunglasses shaded the exact pink of her bikini. "She can take care of herself."

"I hope so," Elizabeth muttered.

But if that was true, why did she have this gnawing feeling in the pit of her stomach that this time dear Jessica was definitely in over her adorable but careless little head?

Two

"You should have seen the look on my dorm mother's face when she caught Bobby sneaking out of my room the other morning. She actually asked him what he was *doing* there. As if it wasn't as plain as the nose on her face!"

Sprawled on her back on the lake's sandy beach, Jessica eavesdropped on the conversation that bubbled around her as enticingly as champagne. She felt distinctly out of place, despite her efforts to appear as bored and sophisticated as the other girls. She kept her eyes shut, pretending to be asleep, until one of them poked her in the ribs and asked to borrow her suntan lotion.

In her chamois bikini and cornrowed blond

hair, the girl was a dead ringer for Bo Derek. Jessica couldn't recall her name. Erica something. The beads in her braids clicked and sparkled in the sunlight as she shook her head over some new boyfriend-related disaster.

"Listen, let me tell you about the time Rod and I spent the weekend camping up in the mountains and we got lost. I'd told my mother I was spending the night with Sarah, only she called up and found out I wasn't there. . . ."

Jessica hooked one leg over her strategically bent knee and shifted slightly to a more flattering pose, just in case Scott or one of the other boys happened to be looking. In her new red string bikini she was a match even for "Ms. 10," if she did say so herself. Noisy laughter and splashing reminded her that most of the party's male members were still in the water. Scott had wanted Jessica to go swimming with him, but she'd declined. She wasn't about to get her hair wet or spoil her makeup.

"Have you been seeing Scott for very long?"

The question had been directed at Jessica by a tall, leggy blonde named Greta. Her smallish brown eyes were heavily outlined with charcoal eye pencil, making her nose seem longer than it really was. She reminded Jessica of a guinea pig she'd once had.

"Long enough," she answered, flipping over

onto one elbow. She didn't want them to know that this was their first date.

What would they think if they knew she was the tiniest bit afraid of Scott? Actually, it was a thrilling kind of fear—the way she felt about breaking the speed limit, for instance. She remembered the way Scott had rested his hand against her bare leg in between shifting gears as they were driving up to the lake. Every once in a while he had taken a swig from the beer can tucked between his knees. His hand was cold and wet when he touched her, giving her overheated skin a delightful shock. Without knowing how to explain it, she'd felt distinctly grown-up but at the same time somewhat uneasy—a feeling unfamiliar to her.

"Bo Derek" cast Jessica a sly look. "Just a word of warning where Scott's concerned. I'm not sure how much of it's actually true, but around campus he's got quite a reputation."

A reputation for *what*? Jessica wanted to ask, but at that moment a shadow fell over her, followed by a sprinkle of cold water.

"Did I hear my name mentioned? You ladies are going to have to stop fighting over me and accept the fact that I'm taken."

Scott sank down beside Jessica and draped a wet arm about her shoulders. "For today, anyway," he added and winked.

Jessica shivered, grateful nevertheless for hav-

17

ing been rescued. She angled her chin downward in the sloe-eyed smile she'd been practicing in the mirror lately. Scott *was* cute—even if he was conceited. His eyes were the same metallic blue as the lake and had a slightly devilish glint in them. Droplets of water clung to his mustache, and his hair stood out in dark, wet ringlets. He was no more muscular than boys her own age who worked out with weights in the gym, but there was a manlike hardness to his bronzed build she found dangerous and exciting.

"Watch out, honey, you've caught yourself a live one," Greta warned and gave a tinkling laugh.

"Jessica can handle herself," said Scott. "Can't you, Jess?"

He nibbled at her earlobe. His mustache tickled the inside of her ear. He brushed his fingertips down her spine, hooking a thumb suggestively over her bikini strap. Jessica wasn't sure she liked his assured possessiveness. Except for Bruce Patman, she'd always been the one to call the shots with her boyfriends. She liked the feeling of power it gave her to lead them on, then whirl away with a careless laugh over her shoulder just when they thought they had her. She had a feeling it wouldn't be that easy with Scott. He was more mature and experienced. But that made it a challenge—and, above all else, Jessica loved a challenge.

"Sure I can handle myself," she teased, flicking one long, ruby-frosted fingernail against his cheek. "But I'd rather have you do it."

The joke had the intended effect of making her seem as sophisticated as the others. Everyone laughed except Scott, who tossed her onto her back with a savage growl, giving her a long, hard kiss. Jessica kicked one slender leg up in the air in mock protest. She felt safe enough in the presence of Scott's friends, but she sensed it wouldn't be so easy fending him off if they were alone.

The other boys were coming in from the water now. Rod Shockley grabbed a couple of beers from the Styrofoam cooler under the trees and tossed one over to Scott.

"Here, Daniels. Looks like you need cooling off." He sent Jessica a long appraising look that drew green darts from the eyes of his girlfriend.

"I was just getting warmed up," Scott grumbled.

Beer fizzed over the top of the can as he popped it open. Jessica squealed and pulled away from him as the icy foam dribbled onto her stomach. She was glad for the excuse to free herself from his disturbing embrace.

Someone had lit a joint and was passing it around. Jessica sipped at the beer Scott had given her, pretending not to notice. Though she hated to admit it, she knew she'd gotten into the fast

19

lane this time—maybe too fast. Not that she couldn't handle it, she told herself. She could handle just about anything. . . .

Pretending a sudden interest in the water as the joint made its way toward her, Jessica drifted down to the lake's edge.

"Just getting my feet wet," she called gaily to Scott over her shoulder. She could feel his eyes on her as she walked, so she gave her hips an added little swing for his benefit—as well as for anyone else who might be watching.

Voices carried down to the water's edge, the speakers no doubt thinking she was out of earshot.

". . . Scott sure likes 'em young. . . ."

". . . gotta watch out for them when they're that age. All tease and no tickle. . . ."

". . . jailbait, if you ask me. . . ."

Frowning, Jessica dug her toes into the wet sand. So her careful little act hadn't fooled them after all. They thought she was just a baby. Well, she'd show them! She could twist any one of those guys around her little finger if she wanted to! Scooping up a handful of mud and pebbles, she strolled nonchalantly back to her towel.

"Oh, Scott . . ." Smiling sweetly, she held out her fist.

He looked up at her with a heavy-lidded expression, the result of several hits of the joint.

He came alive with a jerk, however, when she dribbled ice-cold mud across his chest.

Suddenly he was on his feet, chasing her down the beach. Jessica laughed breathlessly, darting out of his way with a squeal of mock alarm. She doubled back through the shallows as he neared her, splashing him as she ran.

"You little—" he growled when he finally caught up with her. Scooping her up in his arms, he carried her down the beach as she struggled and shrieked.

"Scott," she demanded, "where are you taking me? Put me down this instant! Scott!"

She shot a hopeful glance over his shoulder but saw that no one was likely to come to her rescue. Rod and "Bo" had disappeared into the trees themselves, and the others were absorbed in a new joint that was making the rounds. Not that Jessica was really worried. It was all fun and games. Wasn't it?

"Come on," Scott urged, lowering her to the ground as soon as they'd reached the wooded boundary of the beach. "Let's go for a walk. I know a great place where we can be alone. It's somebody's boathouse, but the people only come up here in the summertime, so we're safe."

Jessica didn't protest as he took her hand and led her down a path strewn with dried pine needles that crackled unpleasantly under her bare feet. She'd teased him into going this far.

21

If she made him go back now, it would look as if his friends had been right about her all along.

"Hey—you're really something, you know that?" Scott hooked his arm about her neck, drawing her close. "I can tell you aren't anything like your sister."

"How can you say that? Liz and I are exactly alike."

"Sure, on the outside. But that's only the gift wrapping. I'm more interested in what's going on inside."

He slipped a hand down the back of her bikini bottom. Jessica slapped it away with a playful swat, more nervous than she was willing to admit, even to herself.

The sun was edging below the treetops by the time they reached the boathouse, after what had been more of a hike than a walk. To Jessica, the waterlogged shack looked dark and creepy, not in the least bit romantic. Inside, it was damp and chilly.

"I'm cold," she said. "Let's go back."

Scott wrapped his arms around her in the marshy-smelling dimness. The slapping of water against a boat hull sounded loud in the stillness.

"Don't worry," he promised huskily. "I'll warm you up."

Suddenly he was kissing her in a way that told her he meant business. Jessica backed away but only succeeded in catching her feet in a jumble of rope and tumbling backward onto a pile of burlap sacking.

"Scott, I—" She held out an arm to ward him off, but he mistook it for an invitation.

He descended upon her like an invading army, tugging insistently at her bikini straps while he devoured her neck. The muscles she'd admired on the beach felt knotted and menacing now, as she lay pinned beneath his bulk. His mouth pressed against hers, hot and openly demanding. Jessica shuddered. *No—not this way*, she thought. She'd always been able to control her boyfriends when she wanted to, but Scott was more of a man than a boy, she realized with rising panic. Someone who wasn't about to take no from a girl who'd led him on.

Three

"Stop it, Scott!" Jessica hissed, pushing against the solid wall of his chest with all her strength. "I mean it. Stop it or I'll—"

"Or you'll what?" Scott pulled back with an expression of disdain. "Scream? Forget it, Jessie baby, this isn't the movies. There aren't any Mounties in these woods."

He loosened the string that tied her bikini top, causing her to clutch her arms over her chest to keep the top from falling off. She decided to try another tack, one that had always worked in the past.

"Hey, come on, Scott," she wheedled, giving him the full benefit of her dimpled smile as she quickly tied the bikini strings. "You know I'm

25

crazy about you, but we really should be getting back. It's almost dark. I've got to be getting home pretty soon."

"Home?" he laughed. "Where did you get the idea I was taking you home tonight? I thought you knew. This party is an all-nighter."

Jessica stiffened, all pretense at beguiling sweetness dropping as abruptly as a rock off a cliff. She bit her lip against the flaming tears that threatened her icy composure. Nothing was going right. Nothing was happening the way she'd planned.

This whole thing was Elizabeth's fault, she decided suddenly. If only Elizabeth had tried a little harder to talk her out of this, she was sure she wouldn't be here.

"I *have* to get home," she demanded, her lower lip edging out in a trembling pout that had never been known to fail as a last-ditch means of getting her way. "If you don't take me home, I'll tell my parents you tried—to—" She couldn't bring herself to finish the sentence.

Scott's only response was a harsh bark of laughter. "Go ahead, Jessie, baby. Tell them. Tell them how you lied to them so you could sneak up here with me. Tell them how you just *happened* to be in a deserted boathouse, practically naked, when I came along and tried to take advantage of you." He shook his head. "Sorry, baby, it just doesn't wash."

Jessica's cheeks burned scarlet with rage and humiliation. "Liz was right about you," she growled at him through gritted teeth. "You really are a creep!"

Scott shrugged. "You know what they say—play with fire and you're going to get burned. So you got a little scorched around the edges. Just be glad it wasn't worse."

Casting her a look of idle disdain, he rose and started for the door.

"Where are you going?" she shrieked, suddenly panicky at the thought of being left alone. It was dark outside, and she hadn't the slightest idea where she was. Even a creep like Scott was better than nothing, she decided. "You can't just leave me here. How will I find my way back?"

"Don't worry, you'll find a way. I have a feeling you can do just about anything you set your mind to, Jessie, baby."

"Scott!" She struggled to her feet, but the rope was still caught about them, and she landed back on her rear with a painful thud. "Come back here. *Scott!*"

It was no use. He didn't care if she got lost in the wilderness. He probably wouldn't care if she died out there, she thought. She tightened the strings of her bikini top, breaking a fingernail in the process.

"Damn," she swore as she freed herself from the rope and ran outside to catch up with Scott.

He was nowhere in sight. She looked for the path, but that, too, seemed to have disappeared in the darkness. Why did all trees have to look so maddeningly alike? How on earth did Scott expect her to find her way out of this rat's maze?

It was all his fault. He'd practically *kidnapped* her, for heaven's sake! It would serve him right if something horrible happened to him on the way back—like stumbling into a bear trap.

At the thought that there might actually be bears in the woods, Jessica experienced a fresh wave of panic. Tingling with goose bumps, she thrashed her way through the underbrush with increased determination, unmindful of the twigs that scratched against her bare legs and arms. She had even forgotten that she was cold.

She wished now that she hadn't dropped out of girl scouts when she was younger. Maybe it would have taught her how to find her way out of a situation like this. Even knowing how to rub two sticks together to make a fire was better than nothing. But she'd told Elizabeth it was only for goody-goodies, and her sister had shrugged and told her to suit herself. Why had Elizabeth let her drop out so easily? She could have convinced her to stay if she'd given it half a try. . . .

By the time Jessica had located some semblance of a path, all her anger was focused on Elizabeth and Scott. She figured her sister *owed* it to her to cover for her. It was the least Elizabeth could do after getting her into this mess. Of course, Jessica knew it would be up to her to provide a convincing excuse for why she was so late. She discarded half a dozen or so before deciding on the tale that sounded most plausible. She would tell her parents that Cara's father's car had broken down on a remote country road, and she couldn't get to a phone. Cara would back her up. She'd better. Jessica would never forgive her if she didn't!

After what seemed like hours, she finally stumbled upon a cabin that looked inhabited. Lights shone in the windows, and loud rock music spilled from the open doorway. A familiar voice greeted her as she groped her way up the front steps.

"Well, well. If it isn't our little lost lamb." Scott emerged from the shadows inside, beer can in hand. His expression had the Silly Putty distortion of intoxication. "What happened, Jessie, baby, did you take a wrong turn back there in the woods?"

She shook him off when he grabbed her elbow with clumsy roughness. Removing a twig from her tangled hair, she tossed it defiantly in his face.

29

Scott pretended to be mortally wounded and staggered backward into the room, falling onto the couch with a snort of drunken laughter.

Jessica looked around for Scott's friends, but judging from the muffled noises coming from the bedrooms, they were obviously far too busy with one another to be concerned with her plight. It looked as though they'd been busy for quite some time. Empty beer cans littered the floor alongside overflowing ashtrays. A table in the corner was piled high with dirty dishes.

"If we'd known you were gonna make it, we would've saved you something to eat," Scott said, not sounding the least bit sorry.

"I'm not hungry," Jessica spat back. The truth was she was starved, but she wouldn't have given him the satisfaction of knowing it. "Where's the phone?" she demanded.

Scott started to giggle as if she'd just said something immensely funny. His head lolled back against the armrest, and his arms flapped weakly at his sides. How could she ever have thought he was good-looking? Something in Jessica snapped. She grabbed him by the shoulders and shook him hard.

"Now you look here, Scott Daniels!" she screamed, two inches from his face. "I'm cold and tired and scratched to pieces, and I'm in no mood for rotten jokes! Either you tell me where the phone is or—or—" She looked wildly about for something to threaten him with. Finally she seized an empty wine bottle from the coffee table and brandished it over his limp form. "Or I'll break this over your stupid head!"

Scott sobered a notch, his drunken laughter replaced by a lopsided grin. "I hope you brought a good pair of hiking shoes, 'cause the nearest phone is a good ten miles down the road."

"Ooooh!" Jessica had a good mind to break the bottle over his head anyway. Damn Scott! Damn Elizabeth! Damn everybody!

Instead, she slumped onto the edge of the couch in momentary defeat. "What am I going to do? My parents are expecting me home. And I have a test tomorrow that I haven't even begun to study for." It was no use pleading with Scott to drive her home. He was too drunk for that now.

Scott's expression held not a flicker of sympathy. "You should've thought of all that before you came," he told her. "But, hey, don't let it get you down, babe. I have a feeling you're used to getting in and out of trouble. I'm sure that pretty little head of yours will come up with something."

"Thanks for your confidence," she flung back at him in disgust. "You're a real winner yourself." An idea came to her all of a sudden, and she smiled. "Listen—I think I left my sweater in the car. If you'll just give me the keys . . ."

31

"No dice, baby. I know what you'd do with those keys if you got your hot little hands on 'em. I'm wise to you, Jess. You know why? 'Cause we're alike, that's why. We want what we want, and we don't care how we get it."

He flashed her a wicked grin. "If you want a ride home bad enough, there's only *one* way of getting it. Otherwise, you'd better find yourself a place to sleep on the floor, 'cause all the beds are taken, and I'm sure as hell not giving up this couch."

"I'd rather sleep with a grizzly bear!" fumed Jessica. "You're the most insufferable creep I've ever met in my entire life. Besides being a conceited jerk, you're the—" She stopped when she saw that he wasn't listening.

Scott's eyes had drooped shut, and his mouth hung slackly open. A loud snore shook his chest. Furious, Jessica plucked the sock that dangled halfheartedly from one of his feet and crammed it into his mouth. Scott sputtered and rolled onto his side, but he didn't give her the satisfaction of waking up.

With a groan of frustration, Jessica surrendered to her fate. She found a place on the floor where she could lie down, then wadded up a beach towel to use as a pillow. Getting to sleep was another matter, she discovered. The floor was hard and uneven. She shivered in the chill draft that swirled down from the chimney. Loud music blared from the next room. Jessica had never been so miserable in her life.

Four

Elizabeth gave a groan and rolled over when the alarm jangled on Monday morning at seven-thirty sharp. *Just a few more minutes,* she pleaded with herself. She'd been dreaming about Todd. The two of them were in the darkroom at school, developing pictures of a beautiful lake. Then he had his arms around her and was kissing her. . . .

When she opened her eyes to peer at the clock again, it was five after eight. She had exactly half an hour to get dressed, eat breakfast, and dash off to school. Yawning, she crawled reluctantly from the warm cocoon of her blankets.

I rose from the warmth of my dreams to the chill

dawn of reality, she made a mental note to write in her journal.

She remembered the tourist-guide test, the reason she was so exhausted. She'd been up half the night studying. The other half was spent worrying about Jessica.

Jessica! Suddenly wide awake, Elizabeth sprinted through the bathroom joining the girls' bedrooms. She groaned when she saw that her sister's bed hadn't been slept in. As she sank down on the bedspread, her stomach executed a slow cartwheel of fear. What if something really terrible had happened to Jessica? What if she'd gotten into an accident? Imprinted in her mind like ugly graffiti were the skid marks left by Scott's tires when he'd squealed away from the curb.

Reason reasserted itself like a splash of cold water. No, she thought, if Jessica had been in an accident they would have heard by now. Her dear sister, Elizabeth was suddenly quite sure, had merely decided she was having too good a time to come home. That would be just like her. She was selfish enough to forget all about Elizabeth and the trouble she was getting them both into. She'd probably even forgotten all about the test.

Well, this is one mess Jessie can find her way out of all on her own! Elizabeth fumed inwardly.

She sighed, realizing in the same instant what

an impossible situation Jessica had placed her in. At this point Elizabeth was in just as deep as her sister. She knew her parents would be angry and upset—and rightfully so—if they knew she'd kept silent about Jessica's whereabouts or the fact that she hadn't come home last night. They'd gone out to dinner and a movie and had assumed Jessica had returned from Cara's while they were away and that she was already asleep. Otherwise, good old dependable Elizabeth would have said something. Right?

Wrong, wrong, wrong. In the bathroom Elizabeth splashed warm water on her face. *How does Jessica always manage to get you into these situations?* she asked the puffy-eyed girl in the mirror. Maybe Enid was right. Maybe she should just let her sister sink or swim the next time. If anyone deserved it, Jessica did. The trouble was that Elizabeth could never seem to stay mad at her for very long. And she couldn't bear just to stand by and do nothing when someone needed her help—especially when that someone was her own sister.

"I should have 'Welcome' tattooed across my chest," she sputtered in disgust through a froth of toothpaste foam.

She was just stepping from the shower when Alice Wakefield called up the stairs that breakfast was ready. "You girls had better hurry up, or you'll be late for school!"

Elizabeth's heart sank at her mother's cheery tone.

"Coming!" she yelled, hoping her mother wouldn't notice that only one of them had answered.

She slid into a pair of old jeans worn to velvety softness and yanked a long-sleeved T-shirt over her head. Quickly she combed her wet hair and secured it with a tortoiseshell clip on either side. She was jamming her feet into a pair of mocassins when the phone rang, nearly causing her to jump out of her skin.

"I'll get it!" she called down to her mother as she dashed to answer the upstairs extension.

"Thank God, Lizzie, I was hoping it would be you!" The panic-filled voice shot out from the receiver.

Jessica. Just as she'd suspected. Elizabeth clutched the phone to her mouth and spoke in an indignant whisper.

"Where on earth *are* you? Do you have any idea—"

Jessica cut her off with a noisy sigh. "Listen, it's a long story. I'll fill you in on the details later. Does Mom know I'm not there?"

"Not yet, but she's about to find out. Jess, we're supposed to be leaving for school in less than fifteen minutes. How do you expect—"

"Please, Lizzie, you've got to help me!" Jessica's voice wavered on the edge of tears. "You can't imagine what I've been through. I—I just don't think I could take it if Mom and Dad found out on top of everything else. . . ."

"What about the test?" Elizabeth demanded.

"I can still make the test if you'll help me. Oh, Liz, I *know* you can. You're the best sister in the whole world. And I'd do the same for you. Honestly I would."

Elizabeth sighed, more out of exasperation than sympathy. "Yeah, right. But just what do you expect me to *do*? I'm not a magician, you know. I can't be two people at once. Mom's going to *know* when you don't come downstairs for breakfast!"

"Oh, I just know you'll think of something," Jessica cooed in her silkiest, melted-butter voice. "You're so smart, Liz."

"If I'm so smart, how come I always get stuck cleaning up *your* messes?"

"I'll make it up to you. Honest, I will. Just help me out this one time, and I'll never ask another favor of you as long as I live. Scout's honor."

"You dropped out of girl scouts, remember?"

"Listen, I've got to go. I'll explain everything when I see you. Oh, and thanks a million!"

Elizabeth realized as she hung up that she still didn't have the slightest idea where her sister was or what catastrophic thing had happened to her. And why was Jessica thanking her when she hadn't even promised to help?

Today I strangled my twin sister, she mentally scribbled in her journal.

No good. She would have to wait until later to strangle Jessica. Right now she had to find a way of getting them both out of this mess.

"Girls!" Alice Wakefield's voice had taken on an impatient edge.

Elizabeth hesitated at the top of the stairs. In her panicked state, she'd drawn a complete blank. What was she going to tell her mother? Like a transmission clicking automatically into second gear, she reverted to an old trick she'd used since childhood on those rare occasions when she needed to find a quick way out of a sticky situation: She imagined she was Jessica.

What would Jessica have pulled out of her bag of magic tricks? She had few of Elizabeth's scruples, so it was usually a case of "anything goes."

Suddenly Elizabeth knew exactly what she had to do. The thought made her positively dizzy, but she could see no other way out. Taking a deep breath, she started slowly down the stairs.

Five

"Where's Jessica?" Alice Wakefield slid a steaming stack of pancakes onto a plate and handed it to her daughter as she entered the kitchen.

"Uh—she'll be down in a minute." Elizabeth kept her eyes glued to the floor. Her hair fell forward in a shining curtain to mask her scarlet cheeks. "She, uh, has to sew a button on her skirt."

"Well, she'd better hurry. I have to be getting ready for work myself in a few minutes. Turning pancakes all morning isn't exactly my idea of gainful employment."

Mrs. Wakefield spoke good-naturedly as she moved briskly between the stove and the butcher-block island that occupied the center of the kitchen's spacious work area. She'd gotten up at dawn to go jogging, as she did every morning, and still was wearing her burgundy velour warm-ups and her running shoes. Her honey-blond hair was caught up in a ponytail, adding a youthfulness to her tanned, slender appearance that made her seem closer to her daughters' age than her own. It was easy to see where the twins had gotten their sun-kissed good looks.

Noting that Elizabeth seemed unusually quiet, Alice Wakefield paused to ask, "Are you worried about that test you're taking today? I know getting that license means an awful lot to you girls."

Elizabeth forced down a forkful of pancakes and syrup, nudging it along with a generous swallow of milk. Normally, pancakes were her very favorite breakfast, but this morning she wasn't a bit hungry. Her stomach felt as if it had been braided.

"Mmmm," she mumbled. "I'm pretty sure I'll do all right. The questions aren't really all that hard; there're just going to be a lot of them. Tons of little facts to remember."

"When I was your age, I wanted to be a camp counselor one summer," her mother mused. "About twenty kids applied, and they only needed five. So we took a test, and then they interviewed us."

"Did you get the job?"

Her mother chuckled. "I failed the test miserably, but the woman who was interviewing us turned out to be someone I did baby-sitting for. She liked me so much that she gave me the job anyway."

"I'll bet you made a great counselor, Mom."

"I'm not sure how great I was, but it certainly was a lot of fun. I'm so glad you and Jess decided to do this. And it's nice you'll be able to work together."

"If we both pass, that is," Elizabeth muttered darkly.

"I *am* a bit worried about your sister. I hope she didn't get home too late to do some studying. Do you know what time she got in?"

Elizabeth choked on the mouthful of pancakes she was swallowing. She doubled over in a fit of coughing that brought her mother scurrying over to deliver a few solid pats on her back.

"My goodness!" her mother cried when Elizabeth's red color had returned to normal. "When will you girls learn to take smaller bites? Every time that happens, you add another gray hair to my head."

Elizabeth smiled; there wasn't a single gray hair among her mother's tawny locks. "Sorry, Mom, I guess I was kind of in a hurry." She wasn't really sorry, though. She'd succeeded in distracting her mother from the subject of Jessica's whereabouts.

Her mother smiled as she shook her head, smoothing a stray wisp from her forehead. "I was just thinking of the fights you and Jess used to have when you were still in high chairs. She would start by throwing pieces of her food at you, and you'd usually wind up dumping your cup of milk over her head." She laughed. "Something you should know in case you're ever blessed with twins someday, Elizabeth—you need double the patience."

"Thanks, but I don't plan on having twins." She didn't add that it was enough trouble just dealing with being a twin.

Her mother laughed. "Neither did I, dear. Neither did I."

A minute later, she frowned and glanced up at the ceiling. "What's taking Jessica so long? I've got to get to work. She should be finished sewing that button on by now."

Elizabeth shoveled in the last of her breakfast with lightning speed. "Thanks for the pancakes, Mom. They were great. I've got to run. I'm meeting Todd."

"What about your sister?" Alice Wakefield called after her as she was going out the door.

"Sorry—can't wait. Tell her I'll meet her later on."

"Oh, well—OK then. Good luck on the test, dear. I know you won't need it, but good luck anyway."

I'm going to need all the luck I can get, Elizabeth thought gloomily as she ducked outside. She'd made it past first base, but she was far from safe. The hardest part was still to come. Could she do it? Could she fool her mother into thinking she was Jessica? She was certain Jessica would have no trouble pulling off the deception—she'd done it often enough in the past. Like the time at Kelly's bar, when she'd let everyone believe she was Elizabeth, nearly costing Elizabeth both her reputation and her budding relationship with Todd. But she didn't want to think about that now. If she stopped to count all the reasons why she shouldn't be doing Jessica a favor, she'd end up sitting outside all day.

Silently cursing her twin, Elizabeth doubled back around the side of the house, crouching down as she passed the kitchen window so her mother wouldn't see her. Carefully, ever so carefully, she let herself in through the front door, removing her mocassins as she did so.

She raced upstairs with her heart in her throat, not daring to breathe until she'd reached the safety of Jessica's room. There, she quickly peeled off her clothes and stuffed them into the closet. Choosing a short, bias-cut skirt and matching striped top that was one of Jessica's favorite outfits, she hastily made the change, pulling the clips out of her hair and giving her head a shake. A dash of her twin's favorite cologne and some of her lipstick and she was ready—if not exactly eager—to go downstairs and greet the world as Jessica Wakefield.

"I swear I'll get you for this, Jess." Elizabeth hissed into the mirror, wagging an exasperated finger at her alter ego's reflection. "If it's the last thing I do!"

Fortunately, Alice Wakefield was already busy with the dishes, and she barely glanced up as Elizabeth swooped into the kitchen and gave her mother a swift, perfumed peck on the cheek.

"Sorry I took so long, Mom. You know me when it comes to sewing." She settled into Jessica's chair. "My hands turn into baseball mitts whenever I get near a needle and thread."

Elizabeth knew her sister so well that the performance was second nature, despite her discomfort at having to give it.

"I'd just about given up on you." Alice Wakefield turned toward her daughter only long enough to set the last of the pancakes in front of her.

Elizabeth groaned inwardly. She was already so full she could scarcely move. Ugh! She could picture the headline in the next edition of *The Oracle*: "Columnist Rushed to Hospital for Stomach Pumping! Condition Critical!"

"Forgive me, stomach, for what I'm about to do to you," she muttered under her breath, courageously spearing a generous forkful. She would have to make a good show of eating to keep her mother from getting suspicious. Unfortunately, pancakes also happened to be Jessica's favorite breakfast.

Mrs. Wakefield spoke over her shoulder as she loaded the dishwasher. "Liz couldn't wait. She said she'd meet you later on."

"No problem," Elizabeth replied with an airy wave of her hand. "She's probably meeting Todd anyway. I'll catch up with her at school."

She chattered on, scarcely taking a breath between bites. She didn't want to give her mother an opening to ask about her day with Cara. "Oh, by the way, did you get a chance to look at that blouse I was telling you about? The one in the window of Foxy Mama?" Elizabeth remembered overhearing Jessica telling their mother about the blouse the other day.

Mrs. Wakefield sighed. "Honestly, Jess, you need a new blouse like I need triplets. If you ever bothered to wash and iron the ones at the bottom of your closet, you could probably double your wardrobe."

Elizabeth rolled her eyes at the thought of the laundry—the twins' responsibility ever since their mother had gone back to work a few years ago.

47

Elizabeth was about to plead for the blouse again when she was struck by a sudden bolt of inspiration. The corners of her mouth lifted in an impish smile.

"You should get it for Liz," she suggested sweetly. "She never asks for anything. At least then I could borrow it once in a while."

"You're absolutely right. Elizabeth *doesn't* ask very often. You could take a lesson or two from her in that department. As for the blouse . . . we'll see. I'm not sure Elizabeth's tastes run as much toward the outlandish as yours. Though I must say," she added with a quick smile, "you look very nice this morning."

Elizabeth was halfway out the door when her mother called after her, "Oh, Jess—"

Elizabeth froze, certain she'd been given away by some minor detail she'd overlooked in making her hasty transformation. She was sure her mother could hear the way her heart was hammering.

"I just wanted to wish you good luck on the test. I doubt if you got in as much studying as you should have, but I'm sure you'll do just fine."

"Uh, yeah, sure," Elizabeth stammered. "Bye, Mom."

She fled down the driveway as if she were being chased. She'd pulled it off—but at what cost? She was sick about deceiving her mother. What had possessed her to ask for that blouse? And her stomach felt as if she'd swallowed the Goodyear blimp.

Strangling was too good for Jessica, she decided.

Six

The smell of freshly mowed grass was the first thing that greeted Elizabeth as she trudged up the sloping front lawn of Sweet Valley High. It was a perfect spring day. A cloudless blue sky spanned the roof of the sprawling red brick school building. Sunlight glinted off the curlicued brass hands of the giant Romanesque clock that dominated the school's impressive white-columned facade.

"Enid!" Elizabeth called out after her best friend, who was on her way through the double doors ahead.

Enid glanced over her shoulder at Elizabeth but didn't stop.

Elizabeth was out of breath by the time she

caught up with her friend at their lockers. "Why didn't you wait?" she gasped.

Enid gave her a funny look. "I guess I just couldn't imagine what you would have to say to me, Jessica," she replied coolly.

"Jessica?" For a moment Elizabeth had forgotten. "Enid—it's me, Liz!"

"Oh, my gosh, Liz!" Enid clapped a hand over her open mouth. "I'm sorry. How could I have thought—?" She stopped, her eyes narrowing. "Wait a minute, that's not your outfit. It's Jessica's. What are you doing in her clothes?"

Elizabeth sighed. "It's a long story." She gave Enid a quick rundown on this latest Jessica-inspired disaster. "The question is, where is Jessica now? I don't even know what happened to her last night."

Enid bit her tongue to hold back the scathing remark she'd been about to make. "Some of those college parties can get pretty wild, from what I hear. Remember that pajama party my cousin told us about? Jessica probably just had too much to drink and passed out or something." She smiled to herself, thinking of the miserable hangover Jessica would be suffering as a result.

"Maybe you're right." Elizabeth wouldn't have put such a thing past her sister. "I guess it doesn't really matter at this point. The only thing that worries me now is the test. What if Jess doesn't show up when it's her turn to take it?"

Enid shrugged. "That's her problem, if you ask me."

"Jessie's not really as tough as she seems," Elizabeth remarked doubtfully.

"Oh, she'll manage somehow. She always lands on her feet—no matter how much trouble she's gotten herself into."

Elizabeth looked so miserable that Enid couldn't resist putting an arm around her shoulders.

"The trouble is," Elizabeth went on, "I'm in this, too—whether I want to be or not. I promised Jessica I'd help." She gave a sheepish grin. "Well—sort of."

"I can imagine." Enid removed her chemistry notebook and a dog-eared copy of *Macbeth* from her locker.

"It's not just Jessica I'm thinking of, either," Elizabeth was quick to point out. "We planned on being tourist guides *together*. No matter how mad I get at Jess sometimes, it just wouldn't be the same without her. It's for *me*, too."

"I'm sure it'll work out," Enid told her, though secretly she had her doubts. "When's the test?"

"I'm taking mine right now, but Jessica's isn't scheduled until second period."

"That's an hour away. Don't worry. She's got plenty of time."

Elizabeth chewed her lip. "I'm not so sure—knowing Jessie. We have this joke in our family that the reason she was born four minutes later than me was because she forgot to put on her watch. Gosh, I don't think Jess even *owns* a watch."

"If the test is as important to her as it is to you, she'll find a way to get here on time," Enid said.

"I wish I could believe that," Elizabeth muttered, her words drowned by the deafening clang of the first bell.

She spent the next few minutes scouring the corridors for some trace of her twin. No one had seen her, though several people did double takes, mistaking Elizabeth for Jessica. Even Bruce Patman was fooled.

"Hey, babe," he called out loudly as she breezed past him, flashing her his famous heart-breaker smile. Some time back Jessica had met her match in gorgeous, arrogant Bruce, until their fiery romance had exploded. But that was old news by now, and recently he'd been trying to worm his way back into her good graces. "How about going out with me this Saturday night?"

"Not a chance," Elizabeth tossed back cheerfully. It was exactly what Jessica would have wanted her to say. For the first time that day, Elizabeth didn't mind playing her twin's double.

She spied Todd a short way down the corridor talking to Bill Chase and angled toward him.

"Liz?" he asked hesitantly.

Elizabeth grinned. "Yeah, it's me."

"Did I hear what I thought I heard? Was that Bruce Patman asking you out?" Todd demanded, breaking away from his conversation with Bill Chase to join her. "Talk to you later," he yelled after Bill, who was already shuffling off toward class. Turning back to Elizabeth, he threatened, "One of these days I'm going to annihilate that creep."

"Who—Bill?" Elizabeth asked distractedly.

"Naw, I meant Bruce. What was he doing asking you out, anyway?"

"Oh, that. Don't worry. He wasn't asking me out. He was asking Jessica."

"Well, there *is* something awfully 'Jessica' about you today," Todd said, a note of confusion in his voice.

No response.

Todd passed a hand in front of Elizabeth's eyes as if he'd caught her in a trance. "Are you sure you're feeling OK? You didn't get hit over the head or anything, did you?"

"That's one way of looking at it, I suppose," Elizabeth replied with a giggle.

"OK, be mysterious." He looked mysteriously happy about something himself, she thought. "Nothing could spoil the good mood I'm in today." He waited a beat, an irrepressible grin

55

plastered across his face. "Aren't you even going to ask me why I'm in such a terrific mood?"

"Why are you in such a terrific mood, Todd?" Elizabeth asked dutifully.

"Because I finally have enough money to buy that Yamaha I was telling you about. Man, I can hardly wait." He closed his eyes in an expression of rapture. "I can almost feel the breeze whistling past my helmet now."

"That's—that's great, Todd."

For a minute Elizabeth's worries about Jessica were sidetracked by a brand-new dilemma. Her parents had absolutely forbidden her ever to ride on a motorcycle. It was one of their strictest rules. What was she going to tell Todd? She pushed it to the back of her mind for the present. He hadn't even gotten the motorcycle yet. She would cross that bridge when the time came.

"Hey," he asked her, coming to earth again, "are you really OK? You look a little spaced out. Is it that test you're worrying about?" He placed a concerned arm about her shoulders.

"Oh, Todd . . ." Burying her head against the welcome haven of his shoulder, she spilled out the entire story.

Todd grew silent, and Elizabeth could tell from the way he was looking at her that he disapproved. Finally he said in a quiet voice, "You shouldn't let Jessica get away with so much, Liz. She just uses you."

"I know I shouldn't, but she's my sister. I can't just stand by and do nothing."

"Look," Todd said, his face showing the strain of remaining neutral where Jessica was concerned, "there's no real harm done so far. And you've certainly done everything you could. Nobody, not even Jessica, could ask for more. So forget about her for now. Go take the test. I'm sure you'll pass with flying colors." He kissed her lightly on the mouth. He smelled faintly of toothpaste and the spicy aftershave he used.

"I guess there's not much else I can do." She kissed him back. "Thanks, Todd."

Smacking his lips with exaggerated relish, he replied, "Thank *you*—Jessica. You kiss almost as well as your sister."

Elizabeth tried to punch him, but laughing wickedly, he ducked out of the way.

By the time she reached the classroom where she was to take the test, Elizabeth had nearly succeeded in banishing her worries about Jessica. Still basking in the glow of Todd's love, she sailed through the test. A lot of the questions had been worded to be deliberately confusing, but Elizabeth had no trouble sorting them out. She was one of the first to hand her answers in to Miss Bascombe, the teacher monitoring the first-period test.

"*There* you are." Cara swooped down on her from out of nowhere as she was leaving the classroom. I've been looking absolutely every-where for you, Jessica Wakefield."

She clutched Elizabeth's arm, lowering her voice to a shrill whisper. "You're not getting away from me until I've heard everything, I mean *everything*, about the party."

Elizabeth smiled sweetly, her blue-green eyes sparkling with mischief. "Gosh, Cara, I don't know where to begin. . . ."

Seven

Cara had Elizabeth's arm in a clinch that would have made a wrestler wince.

"I don't *believe* it." Her dark eyes were wide with incredulity. "You actually told Scott off in front of all his friends?"

"That's not all," Elizabeth continued in a conspiratorial tone. She was really beginning to enjoy this. It wasn't often her flair for storytelling was given such free rein. "Scott was acting like such a creep while we were rowing around the lake that I pushed him overboard."

"You didn't! With all his clothes on?"

"Every stitch."

"Jessica, you are *evil*." Cara beamed with undisguised admiration. "I'll bet he deserved it,

59

too. Men can be such jerks sometimes. How did he act afterward?"

Elizabeth giggled. "Ever see that old movie, *Creature from the Black Lagoon*?"

Cara dissolved into gales of laughter. "Oh, I wish I'd been there. I'd give anything to have seen that!"

So would I, Elizabeth thought wickedly, as she conjured up a picture of Scott with algae dripping from his mustache. He had to be a good part of the reason Jessica hadn't come home last night.

Why hadn't Jessica listened to her when she warned her Scott was trouble? Elizabeth sighed. In Jessica's eyes that probably only made him more attractive.

Over Cara's shoulder she caught sight of Todd ambling toward them. She made a gesture with her hand to let him know she didn't want her cover blown. Todd winked knowingly and placed a finger to his lips in response. His brown eyes twinkled with suppressed amusement as he lazily looped an arm about Elizabeth's slender waist.

"Hiya, Jess. You know something? You're beginning to remind me more of your sister every day."

"Flattery will get you everywhere," Elizabeth purred, fluttering her eyelashes at him.

With an expression of puzzled delight on her

face, Cara looked from one to the other. Everyone knew that Todd had once been a source of competition between the two sisters. Elizabeth figured the gossip would be bounding off the walls by the time she got to PE that afternoon. She coughed loudly to disguise the laughter that bubbled up in her throat.

Elizabeth could see that Cara was also dying to know more about the wild party at the lake but didn't want to pump her further in front of Todd.

Cara cast a meaningful look at her, reluctantly saying, "Well, I guess I'd better get going. I have a history quiz next period, and I haven't even *glanced* at last night's homework assignment."

Todd laughed. "Don't look at me. My knowledge of history is limited to what happened last week."

"I'm sure you'll knock 'em dead, Cara," Elizabeth responded.

"Bye, you two." Cara spotted Lila Fowler and was off like a shot, waving a bangled wrist. "Oh, *Li-la* . . ." she sang out.

Elizabeth giggled. "I'll bet one of Cara's ancestors was a town crier. What do you want to bet the whole school will be buzzing with the news by lunchtime?"

"What news is that?" asked Todd.

Briefly she told him the story she'd made up

about Scott. "It'd serve him right if Jess *had* pushed him overboard," she said. "The first time I laid eyes on him, I knew he'd end up getting her in trouble."

"You make Jessica sound like an innocent bystander," Todd commented dryly. "I wonder what *she* was doing all the time Scott was leading her astray with his evil ways."

Elizabeth frowned, a note of annoyance creeping into her voice. "You don't have to be sarcastic about it." The strain of Jessica's absence was beginning to wear on her nerves.

"I take it Little Red Riding Hood hasn't shown up yet," Todd surmised.

"Not yet," Elizabeth replied defensively. She darted a nervous glance at the clock above the multi-use room. In keeping with her Jessica impersonation, she hadn't put on her wristwatch when she got dressed.

"There's nothing you can do about it one way or the other," he told her. "Why not forget it?"

Elizabeth chewed her lip and frowned up at the clock once again.

Todd knew that expression. He seized both of Elizabeth's hands, forcing her to meet his gaze. "If you're thinking what I think you're thinking, *don't*, Liz. You can't take that test for Jessica. That would be the same as cheating. I know you—you wouldn't dream of cheating for yourself, so why do it for Jessica?"

"It wouldn't *really* be cheating," she defended weakly.

Nonetheless, she felt sick about what she was contemplating. There was a sour taste in the back of her mouth, and her head was starting to ache. It was like quicksand, she thought. The harder you tried to get out, the deeper you sank.

"What would you call it?" challenged Todd.

"Jess knows the answers. I'm sure she'd pass if she were here."

"That's just the point, don't you see? She isn't here. Come off it, Liz. When are you going to stop taking all the knocks for Jessica's irresponsibility? Do you really think she'd do the same for you?"

"That's unfair!" Elizabeth shot back, partly because she was tired and upset, partly because she knew, deep down, that he was right. She couldn't imagine Jessica doing all this for her if the situation had been reversed.

"You're just saying that because you don't like her," she accused. "You've never liked her."

Todd lifted an eyebrow in surprise. "I guess it should be obvious to you, of all people, why I'm not so crazy about your sister."

Back when Elizabeth and Todd were first getting together, Jessica had wanted him for herself.

She had tried to stop her sister's blossoming romance, but for once her devious tricks had failed. In fact, all she had succeeded in doing was winning Todd's permanent distrust. He wouldn't easily forget the way she'd selfishly tried to manipulate his feelings—and Elizabeth's as well.

"In my opinion Jessica cares more about herself than anyone else," he added.

Elizabeth whirled on him, her eyes bright with angry, unshed tears. "Who asked you for your opinion, anyway?"

He touched her arm. "Look, I was only trying to—"

"I know what you were trying to do!" she cried, shaking his hand off. "You were trying to turn me against my own sister! I never thought you'd stoop so low, Todd Wilkins."

A dull flush crept up the sides of his neck. It was the first time they'd ever argued. He looked as if someone had delivered a karate chop to his stomach.

"I'm sorry you feel that way," he answered stiffly. "I was only trying to help, Liz. But I guess you just aren't interested in hearing the truth."

"The truth is you're jealous because I'm doing something for Jessica."

"Don't be an idiot!" Todd growled, losing his temper at last.

"So now I'm an idiot on top of being a cheat? Well, you're right about one thing," she said through clenched teeth. "Only an idiot would go out with you!"

Todd looked as if she'd slapped him. "I guess that means our date for Saturday is off," he said coldly.

Saturday was the day of the surfing championship, when half the school would turn out on the beach for an afternoon of wave-watching and sunshine and a giant barbecue after nightfall. Elizabeth wouldn't have dreamed of missing it. And until that moment she wouldn't have dreamed of going without Todd, either. The angry words tumbled out even before she was fully aware of what she was saying.

"I'd rather go swimming with Jaws!" she choked.

"Fine—if that's the way you want it." Todd glowered darkly at her before spinning on his heel and stalking off.

Watching his stiffly held, muscular back retreating down the hallway, Elizabeth immediately felt a sharp pang of regret. She didn't really know why she'd said all those awful things to Todd. They weren't even true. She realized he'd only been trying to help. But where Jessica was concerned, it seemed everything had a way of getting turned hopelessly inside out. Including Elizabeth's own feelings.

She fought the urge to run after Todd. She'd probably just end up making things worse if she tried to apologize now. Swallowing against the tears in her throat, she made her decision. She would have to take the test for Jessica. She'd gone too far to back out now.

Eight

"Maybe it's not as bad as you think," Enid offered sympathetically.

Elizabeth dabbed at her swollen, red eyes with a wet paper towel. "It's worse! I was so upset I could hardly think straight. I just *know* I flunked."

The second version of the test had probably been no harder than the one she'd taken earlier, even though the questions were worded differently. But as far as Elizabeth was concerned, it might have been written in Greek. The words swam about on the paper, blurred by her tears. No matter how hard she tried to concentrate, all she could think about was Todd and the closed expression on his face before he'd walked away.

She'd been the last one to hand her answers in. She vaguely remembered Mr. Sandalow, the second-period test monitor, calling out Jessica's name as she scurried from the classroom in tearful disgrace. Elizabeth had pretended not to hear so she wouldn't have to stop and explain. It was all so complicated by now that she wasn't sure she understood it herself.

"I've ruined everything!" she wailed.

"I'd say you had a little help," Enid noted. She didn't mention any names, but her meaning was clear.

They were in the girls' room, where Enid had found her after the test, crying her eyes out. Elizabeth stared with disgust at her ravaged reflection in the mirror. Her face was a funny blotchy pink, her eye makeup ran in muddy rivers down her cheeks.

"Look at me," she said sniffling. "I'm a mess."

Enid nodded gravely, handing her a fresh paper towel. "I won't argue with that."

"Thanks a lot!"

"Don't worry, you're still gorgeous. Just a little on the messy side right now. Rinse your face, and here"—she dug into her oversize canvas purse—"put on some lipstick and brush your hair. You'll feel better." She handed Elizabeth a comb and a small pot of strawberry lip gloss. "It's not the end of the world, you know."

"Maybe not, but it's the end of Todd and me.

It's the end of my summer, too. If Jessica doesn't pass, it'll spoil everything."

"Seems like *she* should have been the one to think of that before she got you mixed up in all this. At least this way there's a chance she passed the test. She would've flunked for sure if you hadn't taken it for her."

"Somehow knowing that doesn't make me feel any better."

"Look," Enid said, "I was reading this article the other day where it said if you're depressed you should try to think about something *really* awful, like starving people in India or something, and then your own problem won't seem so humungous."

Elizabeth shot her friend a disgusted look. "Thanks a lot. Now I'm really miserable."

"Sorry. I was only trying to help."

"That's what Todd said." Her lips were quivering as she applied a thin coating of gloss.

"What did you do? Bite his head off?"

"Practically. Oh, Enid," she choked, "I really blew it! He'll never speak to me again. I just know it!"

"I wouldn't be too sure of that if I were you. He's pretty hung up on you, in case you haven't noticed lately."

"You weren't there. You didn't see the way he *looked* at me. Like I'd stabbed him, or something. It's all my fault. . . ."

"Come on, you can't take all the blame." Enid's wide green eyes met hers in the mirror. "I won't say again whose fault *I* think it is. I don't want you to bite my head off, too. I may need it for the test on *Macbeth* I'm taking next period."

Elizabeth's laugh emerged as a hiccup. "Don't try to cheer me up. It won't work. I'm too depressed."

"Remember what you told me when I was so miserable about breaking up with Ronnie?"

Elizabeth shook her head.

"You said that if a guy *really* likes you, he won't let a misunderstanding get in the way. Not for long, anyway."

"I don't see how Todd could have misunderstood," Elizabeth replied brokenly. "I told him I'd rather go swimming with Jaws than go to the surfing championship with him."

"Uh-oh." Enid rolled her eyes. "You *do* have a way with words. I think you've been masquerading as Jessica a little too long. It's beginning to rub off."

Elizabeth groaned, and Enid patted her shoulder. "OK, OK, I was only kidding."

The bathroom door blew open, admitting a group of giggling sophomores, followed by Dana Larson, lead singer for The Droids, the band that was Sweet Valley High's contribution to the rock scene.

"What time's the funeral?" Dana asked dryly, taking in Elizabeth's sorry appearance and the mound of soggy paper towels on the sink.

Dana was in one of her usual outrageous getups: an oversize t-shirt over a red-striped miniskirt; purple tights; and black suede ankle boots. An enormous gold loop dangled from one pierced earlobe; the other sported a tiny silver star.

"Don't tell me." Peering into the mirror, she smoothed back a strand of her boyishly cut blond hair. "You had a fight with your boyfriend, right?"

"How did you guess?" Elizabeth asked.

"Men are the root of all our problems." Her expression held an air of profound knowledge. "They can lift us up to the clouds one minute, then plunge us into the pits the next. I know. I was hung up on this saxophonist once—I mean *really* gone on the guy."

"What happened with him?" Enid asked.

"Oh, let's just say we had a parting of the ways. He was more interested in playing around with other girls than with his saxophone," she replied and shrugged. "I was really better off without him. You're probably better off without what's-his-name, too."

Elizabeth moaned. The prospect of being without Todd made her feel positively queasy.

"I think I'm going to be sick," she said.

71

* * *

"You look a little green around the gills, Liz," commented Roger Collins, faculty adviser for the school paper. There was concern in his blue eyes. "Are you sure you're all right?"

Elizabeth nodded dumbly, unable to get any words past the frozen lump in her throat. She sat slumped at her typewriter in the roomy second-floor office of *The Oracle*, staring listlessly at the column she was in the midst of preparing.

A New Wrinkle on an Old Wave?

Reigning state surfing champion, Sonny Callahan, boasts he'll hold on to that title come Saturday, but local experts contend the "Chase" is far from won. Though our own Bill Chase has been mysteriously mum on the subject, his fans predict he'll be riding high into the sunset. . . .

Mr. Collins bent his strawberry-blond head down to scan what she'd written. "Mmmm. Good stuff. How would you like to cover the story on Saturday?"

Elizabeth glanced up in surprise. "I thought John was doing it." John Pfeifer was the sports editor, so naturally she'd assumed . . .

"John told me this morning that he won't be able to make it. They're holding a tennis tournament at the country club the same day. The Patmans are sponsoring it, and I gather Bruce will be playing."

"Naturally," Elizabeth put in.

"I guess you know Mr. Patman is chairman of the school board. He passed down the word that he'd be pretty upset if coverage of a legitimate sports event got preempted by a bunch of, quote, long-haired bums in seal suits, unquote." He grinned. "I wouldn't put that in writing, though, if I were you."

"Don't worry, I won't." Elizabeth had had enough experience with the Patmans, who considered themselves the feudal lords of Sweet Valley, to know better than to cross swords with them.

"Anyway," Mr. Collins continued, "if you want the assignment, it sounds like a good excuse to soak up some sun if nothing else. You game?"

Elizabeth didn't like the idea of going without Todd, but this was in the line of duty. Nothing, not even a broken heart, deserved more attention than her efforts as a journalist and writer. Besides, she didn't want to let Mr. Collins down. He was always there for her when she needed him. He was so sensible, so sincere—not to

mention so handsome—Elizabeth could understand why he was the favorite faculty member
of so many of the students at Sweet Valley
High.

"All right. You can count on me," she said.

"Hey, are you sure you're OK?" Mr. Collins
pressed. "You really do look pale. Why don't
you let me give you a ride home? You look like
you need to lie down."

"It's probably nothing," Elizabeth mumbled,
unable to meet his gaze. "Maybe I just need
some fresh air. Thanks for the offer, but I think
I'll just walk."

She grabbed her books and started for the
door, afraid that if she said any more, she would
start blubbering again. On her way out she
collided with Olivia Davidson, bearing the latest
articles for *The Oracle*'s arts page, of which she
was editor. Immediately they were both caught
in a blizzard of typewritten columns.

"Sorry, Liv!" Elizabeth squeaked, kneeling
awkwardly to help Olivia retrieve the pages.
"I—I guess I didn't see you."

"Hey, don't worry about it." Olivia grinned
good-naturedly, her brown curls peeping out
from underneath a vibrant purple scarf. "I was
looking for a good excuse to drop the project
anyway—pardon the pun. By the way," she
chattered on as she picked up typewritten sheets,

"I just saw Todd out in the hallway. He looked pretty down about something. In fact, if he was any more down, we'd have to get him a stretcher. What's with him, anyway?"

"We had a fight," Elizabeth confessed, and saying the words brought her to the verge of a fresh outbreak of tears.

"Oh, is that all? I thought maybe it was a nuclear holocaust from the way he was acting."

Olivia was big on things like antinuke rallies and organic food. She was always lecturing the newspaper staff—in a nice way—about eating too much refined stuff. Her lunches invariably consisted of things like whole-grain bread, meatless spreads, and alfalfa sprouts. She had a loony sense of humor, though, which Elizabeth enjoyed.

"It might as well be as far as we're concerned," she said.

"That bad, huh? I know what you mean. I had a fight with my boyfriend last week, and we're still not speaking." She sighed. "I guess I knew it was doomed from the beginning. How can I have a meaningful relationship with someone who believes in offshore drilling?"

Elizabeth retrieved the last article from the floor, handed it to Olivia, and fled. She liked Olivia, but she was in no mood to discuss nuclear holocausts and offshore drilling.

She was making her way across the front lawn when she spied a familiar figure in the distance. With a flash of sun-gold hair and a frantic wave, Jessica came bounding toward her.

Nine

"I've never been so humiliated in my whole life!" Jessica shrieked. "You wouldn't believe what a creep Scott turned out to be. I wouldn't go out with him again if he was the last—" She stopped, her eyes widening as if seeing her sister for the first time.

"What are you doing in my outfit?" she asked.

"I—" Elizabeth opened her mouth to explain, but Jessica never gave her the chance.

Instantly she swooped down on her twin with a rib-crushing embrace, as if she'd just won the final round of *The Price Is Right*, and walked away with a Cadillac, a color TV, and an all-expenses-paid trip to Hawaii.

"Oh, Lizzie, I knew it! I just knew you'd find

a way to fix it. You're the best, smartest sister in the whole wide world. I knew you'd find a way to fix it so I wouldn't flunk the test!"

"About the test, Jess—"

"Don't worry, I'll make it up to you somehow. You don't know what this means to me, Liz. I was so sure that goon Scott had ruined my entire summer. You practically saved my life!"

Suddenly Elizabeth didn't have the heart to tell her. She didn't even have the heart to be really mad at her anymore. Jessica would learn the bad news soon enough, when the test scores were posted. Until then Elizabeth could still hold on to the dim hope that maybe, by some miracle, she'd managed to pass the exam for both of them.

Jessica's face shone with happiness, every trace of her miserable ordeal at Scott's hands wiped away as if it had never happened. She didn't even seem to notice that Elizabeth didn't share her exuberance.

"What's with *him*?" Jessica wanted to know, a tiny frown puckering her brow as she directed her gaze at someone over her sister's shoulder. "If looks could kill, I'd say we were both on the critical list."

Elizabeth whirled about in alarm, just in time to see Todd scowling at them as he strode rigidly past. Her heart sank, even as her hand lifted automatically in a little half-wave that froze in midair when confronted by Todd's icy stare. She blinked back tears, ducking her head quickly so he wouldn't notice them.

"Did you two have a fight or something?" Jessica asked, but before Elizabeth could answer, Jessica's attention had been diverted by other, more important matters. "Hey, what time is it, anyway? I think I'm supposed to meet Cara and Lila to go over the new cheer we did in practice yesterday."

"But you missed all your classes," Elizabeth said. "What if you run into one of your teachers?"

"Never mind about them," Jessica said impatiently. "I'll just tell them I was sick or something. It's not exactly a lie." She let a tiny smile lift the corners of her mouth. "That Scott really *did* make me sick."

Jessica glared up at the school clock in disgust, as if it, too, had somehow conspired to cheat her. "Look, Liz, honey, I've got to run. I have to change into my cheerleader stuff. Take it easy, huh?" she called as she dashed off to the gym.

To Elizabeth, in her dismal state, it sounded as ridiculous as the captain of the *Titanic* telling its passengers not to get upset over a little thing like sinking. She'd just lost two of the most important things in her life: Todd and her own self-respect.

How on earth was she going to get them back?

She certainly couldn't count on Jessica's help. Dear, dependable Elizabeth had come through once again, saving her sister from disgrace and disaster. The fact that she'd quite possibly ruined her own life in the process wasn't going to cost Jessica a night's sleep.

"You're a celebrity!" Cara bubbled, rushing over to Jessica in the locker room just as she was zipping up the back of her pleated, blue-and-white cheerleader's costume.

"I am?" Jessica replied, arching her brow.

"I've been telling everyone how you showed Scott up at the party. You're practically the Scarlett O'Hara of Sweet Valley High!"

"What exactly *have* you been telling everyone?" Jessica asked innocently. "Just so I know you haven't left out any important details."

"Don't worry," Lila Fowler put in as she struggled in vain with her own zipper. "She probably invented most of it. She's been blabbing to absolutely *everyone*." Quickly she recounted what Cara had told her. "Now, will someone please help me with this darned thing? I think I've got a thread stuck in it."

Jessica reached over, freeing the zipper with a deft yank. Her blue-green eyes glittered with secret amusement. A smile played at her lips. This wasn't turning out so badly after all.

"You know what they say," she drawled. "Hell hath no fury like a woman scorned." In this case, of course, it didn't hurt to have a twin with a good imagination.

"I'll bet Scott never thought hell would turn out to be so wet!" Cara laughed, sending them all into gales of uncontrollable giggling.

When they arrived at the gym, Jessica sidled up to link arms with Ken Matthews, who was just leaving. Physically, Ken was all you would expect of someone who was captain of the football team: tall, blond, blue-eyed, and gorgeous. Right now he was also sweaty from football practice, and his jersey clung to his broad chest in dark, wet patches. Jessica thought he looked very sexy.

"How's it going, Ken doll?" she flirted. It was an old joke between them; she was always kidding him about his resemblance to Barbie doll's companion.

"Hot," he teased right back, squeezing her arm against his side, "and getting hotter all the time." He grinned down at her. "What's up with you? You look like the cat who ate the canary."

"You could say that," she replied with a wink. "You could definitely say that."

Ten

It was turning out to be the longest week of Elizabeth's life. Each night she found convenient excuses to hover near the phone in the bleak hope that Todd might call. But when it rang, sending her heart leaping into her throat, it was usually Enid, or someone for Jessica.

"You sound disappointed that it's only me," Enid complained on one of these occasions. "You were expecting Princess Di, maybe?"

"Oh, come on, Enid, you know I'm glad to hear from you. It's just that I was sort of, well, you know, hoping . . ." Her voice trailed off in despair.

"Listen, this is getting ridiculous. If Todd hasn't called you, why on earth don't you just call *him*? Someone has to make the first move."

"I already thought of that," Elizabeth replied glumly. "It won't work."

"Why not? How can you say that before you've even tried it?"

"Because I already know what he'd say. Face it, Enid, he's never going to want to speak to me as long as I live."

"Is that what your crystal ball told you?"

"You don't have to make jokes. I'm absolutely serious."

"So am I. How do you know Todd isn't waiting by the phone for you to call him?"

"Because I saw him yesterday in study hall, and he looked right through me as if I were the Invisible Woman or something." Elizabeth sighed. "He didn't even take the trouble to give me a dirty look. It was as if I didn't *exist*. It was awful!"

"Maybe he really didn't see you," Enid offered hopefully.

"Maybe he just didn't *want* to see me."

It was Enid's turn to sigh. "OK, I'm not going to try to convince you. Just remember, when it comes to romance, you don't know how cold the water is until you stick your feet in."

Elizabeth giggled in spite of herself. "Where did you get *that*—out of a fortune cookie?"

"I read it in *Cosmopolitan*, if you want to

know," Enid said defensively. She was a big magazine reader.

"Thanks," Elizabeth said, "but my feet are cold enough as it is. I have a feeling Todd's are, too."

"So what are you going to do?"

"Nothing. Haven't I bungled it enough as it is? Every time I try to fix things, they get even worse."

"I still think it would be better if you went to Todd and told him what you're feeling. Maybe he thinks you're still mad at him. Believe me, being honest is always the best way. Much better than keeping something locked up inside. Look at what that did to me. Not that I'm sorry about the way things turned out, of course. One look at George, and who could be sorry?"

She was referring to George Warren, once a part of her terrible past, but now back in her life in a new and wonderful way.

"That was different," Elizabeth argued.

"Only because it was *me* and not you."

"I think you've been reading *Cosmo* a little too long," Elizabeth commented dryly.

"OK, I can see I'm wasting my breath. Do it your own way. Whatever *that* is," she added pointedly. "And good luck. I have a feeling you're going to need it."

* * *

By Thursday Todd still hadn't called, and Elizabeth was more miserable than ever. She and Enid ran into Cara by the lockers on their way to class. Cara greeted Elizabeth with far less enthusiasm than when she'd mistaken her for Jessica. Nevertheless, she was chatty enough, if for no other reason than that it was a chance to pick up a hot item of gossip.

"I haven't seen you hanging around with Todd lately," she commented, then yawned, as if to emphasize that she couldn't care less. "Is he sick or something?"

Enid nudged Elizabeth with her binder and deftly changed the subject. "Speaking of absences, has anyone seen Bill Chase around lately? He's been absent from my history class for the past three days."

Cara brightened. "You mean you haven't heard?"

"Heard what?" asked Elizabeth.

"The latest word is that Bill Chase is in hiding. *No one's* seen him."

"Hiding from what?" Enid wanted to know. "The FBI?" She giggled. "Somehow I just can't imagine Bill on the Ten Most Wanted List."

"The rumor is that he's avoiding the surfing championship," Cara went on, undeterred by Enid's sarcasm. "I suppose he can't stand the idea of getting slaughtered by Sonny Callahan."

"I don't know," said Elizabeth. "That just

doesn't sound like Bill somehow. I know he seems laid-back and all, but he's pretty involved in this whole thing from what I understand. There's even some surf shop that's sponsoring him, I heard."

Cara's eyes widened at this unexpected tidbit. "Don't you see? That's all the more reason why he should be hiding out. He probably can't bear the thought of facing his sponsor after he gets creamed."

"Sounds pretty drastic to me," Elizabeth said doubtfully. On the other hand, she recalled how glum Bill had looked the previous Sunday at the beach, watching Sonny glide through that curl.

Cara sniffed. "Well, I'm putting *my* money on Sonny. Besides, he's a hunk."

"I think Bill's kind of cute," Enid defended. He wasn't really her type, but she felt obliged to root for him for some reason.

Cara gave her a scathing look. "To each his own," she remarked haughtily as she sailed off toward class.

Elizabeth turned to Enid. "I guess I've been so involved in my own problems I haven't been paying much attention to what anyone else has been doing."

"What can you expect? As if Todd wasn't enough, you have the tour-guide test to worry about, too."

"Every time I think about those scores, I get this awful feeling in the pit of my stomach."

"They're posting the results today, aren't they?" asked Enid.

"After fourth period." Elizabeth groaned.

"Have you told Jessica you're worried?"

"I didn't have the heart. She's been on cloud nine this whole week. Besides, miracles have been known to happen. Maybe she'll pass."

"I can't believe it! I just can't believe it!" Jessica stared at the test results posted on the bulletin board outside the principal's office for several minutes before turning to her sister with a look of despair.

"I—I can't imagine how it happened, Jess," Elizabeth stammered, her cheeks growing pink.

Jessica's eyes remained riveted on her sister's, her expression of agony slowly hardening into one of suspicion.

"*You* passed," she observed, her voice soft but piercing.

"The questions on your test were a little different," Elizabeth offered weakly.

"Yeah, but it was all pretty much the same stuff. They wouldn't make it harder for one group of kids. That wouldn't be fair." Jessica leaned against the wall, one hip slightly forward in a defiant pose. "Liz—how could you *do* this to me?"

"I didn't do anything to you," Elizabeth shot back defensively, starting to feel a little angry herself. "Remember, if you hadn't sneaked off with Scott, you would have been here to take the test yourself. Then you would have had only yourself to blame if you'd flunked."

"I *knew* it!" Jessica jabbed an accusing, ruby-nailed finger at her twin sister. "I knew all along you were jealous. I'll bet you flunked me on purpose, just to get back at me."

"That's an awful thing to say! Besides, why would I be jealous?"

"You were jealous because secretly you wanted to go out with Scott. And all along I thought you were doing me this big favor because I was your sweet baby sister. God, how could I have been so utterly naive!"

"Not naive, Jess," said Elizabeth coldly. "Just plain stupid. If you think I'd care about going out with a creep like Scott—"

But Jessica wasn't even listening. "You did it on purpose," she ranted, staring harshly into Elizabeth's face. "Maybe you didn't plan it that way, but I'll bet you didn't try as hard on my test as you did on yours!"

Elizabeth stared back with a stricken expression. Part of what Jessica said was true, in a weird way. She *hadn't* tried as hard; she'd been too upset. It wasn't on purpose, but the result was the same.

"That's ridiculous," she argued, but her voice lacked conviction. "It wasn't up to me to take the test, anyway. It was *your* responsibility."

"Don't you remember?" Jessica flung back at her, her face contorted with fury. "You promised! You promised you'd help me. And I trusted you. I believed you."

Elizabeth felt herself go white. "I've never done anything to hurt you," she said softly. "I can't believe you'd even think such a thing."

"Oh, don't bother playing sweet, innocent Lizzie with me," Jessica hissed. "If you were so sweet and innocent, you never would have pretended to be me in the first place."

She's right, Elizabeth thought with a dull shock. It had been wrong from the very beginning. She'd known, yet she'd gone ahead with it anyway. Maybe she and Jessica were more alike than she'd ever realized.

Jessica wheeled around in dramatic fury. "I'll never forgive you for this," she directed back at Elizabeth, and her voice was pure ice.

Elizabeth slumped down on the bench outside the principal's office. Her head was buzzing. She was so upset that she actually felt sick. Her mouth was dry, her legs like rubber. She'd only tried to be helpful, and now her life lay in shambles as a result. How had something that had started out as a favor managed to go so terribly, hideously wrong?

Eleven

Elizabeth caught sight of a group of girls she knew heading toward her, and she ducked out a side exit so she wouldn't have to talk to them. She just wanted to be alone—to think, to sort out her feelings. Wrapped in her misery, she drifted off toward the deserted baseball diamond.

She sank down on the empty bleachers, staring blankly at the long, rolling stretches of green. It was quiet except for the distant thwanging of balls hitting the hurricane fences of the tennis courts. The air smelled faintly of the sawdust that had been sprinkled over the diamond. Elizabeth recalled the time she'd sat here, on these bleachers, watching the baseball tryouts. What a day it had been! When Brad Summers hit that

93

fly ball over the bleachers, Todd had seemed simply to reach up and pluck it out of thin air. Everyone had cheered, and she'd been so proud. Later, when he'd kissed her, she'd felt herself soaring up, up, just like that fly ball.

Elizabeth was so caught up in her thoughts, that she didn't notice how late it had gotten. Long shadows crosshatched the field as the sun melted below the horizon. She shivered, hugging her chest, the thin T-shirt she wore no protection against the chill that had crept into the air. Her cheeks were wet and cold with tears she didn't even know she'd shed.

She was startled from her reverie by someone slipping a sweater over her shoulders from behind. She whipped about to find Todd standing over her, looking down at her with a strange, lopsided smile.

"Don't say a word," he ordered in a voice gruff with emotion. "Just shut up and listen, OK?"

Elizabeth nodded, too stunned to argue.

"I've been doing a lot of thinking these past few days, and I've come to the conclusion that we're both a couple of class-A jerks. Since neither of us had the guts to say anything, we probably would've gone on being miserable for the next hundred years. Now don't get any ideas." He held up a hand. "I'm not apologizing.

I think we both said some pretty dumb things. Let's just say I'm calling for a truce. OK?"

"OK." Elizabeth's reply emerged as a squeak.

"Hey, silly, what are you crying for?"

Gently he brushed his forefinger along her cheek. His expression softened to one of open tenderness, his dark eyes taking on a liquid gleam in the fading light.

"Look who's calling who silly," she said, her voice catching a little. But suddenly she couldn't seem to stop grinning.

"I missed you," he said.

"Me, too."

"I'm sorry I—"

"No apologies, remember?"

"OK. So I'm not sorry."

"Me neither."

They were both grinning. A soft breeze nudged a lock of hair over Todd's eye. She reached up and brushed it back.

"You're a mess," he said, digging into his pocket and handing her a crumpled tissue.

"Todd?"

"Yeah?"

"I really can't believe I said all those awful things to you."

"Yeah, well, maybe I deserved some of them. Even if I'm not too crazy about your sister, I should've kept my mouth shut. I'm not too crazy about my *own* sister half the time, but I'd probably waste someone else for badmouthing her."

"I'm not wild about Jessica myself at the moment, if you want to know the truth," Elizabeth confessed.

"I figured that's how it would come down. I saw the test scores. Well, congratulations—at least one of you passed."

"Thanks," Elizabeth said sullenly.

"That bad, huh?"

"She was pretty upset. She really blew up."

"Must run in the family."

He cupped his hands about her face, tipping it up to meet his gaze.

"You were right, Todd," Elizabeth said. "I never should have cheated on that test. I knew it was wrong. That's why I got so angry when you told me off."

"Sure it was wrong, but you did it for the right reasons. You were only trying to protect Jessica. She's your sister, and you love her, no matter what."

"Love does funny things to people."

"Yeah, I happen to have firsthand knowledge of that." He kissed her softly on the forehead, following it with another kiss on the tip of her nose before finally arriving at her mouth.

"What kind of kiss do you call that?" Elizabeth asked when she'd caught her breath.

"A connect-the-dots kiss," he breathed.

"Mmmm, nice."

"This is a shut-up-and-enjoy-it kiss," he continued, brushing his lips against hers.

Wrapped in Todd's arms, surrounded by his clean, warm scent, Elizabeth almost forgot she'd ever been miserable. She snuggled her head against his shoulder, feeling the lean hardness of his muscles beneath his sweat shirt.

"I love you," she murmured.

"Some truce, huh?"

"More like out-and-out surrender."

"On both sides," he was quick to add. "Liz?"

"What?"

"I love you, too."

"I know. Shut up and kiss me, silly."

Todd needed no further invitation.

Twelve

Elizabeth felt as if she were floating two feet off the ground as she and Todd strolled hand in hand back toward the school building. In her blissful fog, she didn't notice they were being pursued until someone snatched her arm from behind, plummeting her abruptly back to earth.

"Liz! Didn't you hear me calling you?" Jessica gasped, out of breath from running. Her cheeks were flushed, her eyes shining with excitement.

Elizabeth stared at her in bewilderment. She was familiar with Jessica's quicksilver mood changes, but this was unbelievable. She felt as if she were on a roller coaster whenever she was around her sister.

"Well?" Elizabeth eyed her with stony coolness. "What is it? Can't you see I'm busy?" She glanced toward Todd, who was eyeing Jessica with suspicion. "I haven't got all day."

"Oh, come off it, Liz," Jessica wheedled. "Don't be like that. Look, I'm sorry I blew up at you. I didn't mean it. You know how I get sometimes."

"Do I ever!"

"I *said* I was sorry. You don't have to get nasty."

"Is that what you ran after me for?" Elizabeth asked impatiently. "To tell me you're sorry?"

"Uh, well, not exactly. Oh, Liz, you'll never guess!" She grabbed her sister by the shoulders, swinging her around. "They're going to give me another chance on the test! Mr. Sandalow called me in and told me he could see how sick I was on Monday and figured that was the reason I did so badly."

Elizabeth felt her anger draining. "Gosh! That's great, Jess." Funny, she thought, how things had a way of working out.

"Great? It's unbelievably fantastic! Isn't it fantastic, Todd?" Jessica gave him a broad smile.

"Fantastic," he echoed, with slightly less enthusiasm.

"I'm really happy for you, Jess," Elizabeth said, hugging her sister back. "And I forgive you—even if you don't really deserve it."

"Oh, you know I never mean any of the

things I say when I get mad. It's just my way of letting off steam. Honestly, I never *really* thought you were jealous about Scott."

"Scott who?" Todd asked, frowning.

"Nobody, silly," Elizabeth reassured him, turning back to Jessica with a scowl. "You'd better quit while you're ahead, or you're *really* going to get me in trouble this time."

Jessica grinned. "My lips are sealed, dear sister."

"I hope your brain isn't. Remember, you haven't passed the test yet. You still have to study."

"Yes, sir." Jessica directed a mock salute at her twin.

"I think all this reconciliation calls for a celebration," put in Todd. "How does a double-decker mocha almond chip at Casey's sound? My treat."

"Great!" Elizabeth responded.

"Sounds delicious," Jessica chimed in enthusiastically. "I'm starved. I've hardly eaten anything today. Not to mention last night—"

"Gee, it's too bad you can't come with us," Todd interrupted, feigning disappointment. But Elizabeth noted the mischievous sparkle in his eyes. "But then I know how it is when you've got a lot of studying to do. Life is full of sacrifices."

Elizabeth giggled. "We'll bring you back

something," she promised. "If it doesn't melt on the way."

"Thanks a lot, you two." Jessica glowered at them. She knew when she'd been out maneuvered.

"Don't mention it!" Elizabeth sang out over her shoulder as she sailed off on Todd's arm.

Thirteen

The beach was packed by the time Todd and Elizabeth arrived on Saturday. Fortunately, Enid and George had saved them a place near the water where the view was relatively unobstructed. They threaded their way toward the ocean through a jungle of splashy-bright beach towels, toasting bodies, and Styrofoam coolers.

It was another perfect, sunny day. The salty air smelled of suntan lotion and surfboard wax, and there was just enough of a breeze to keep everyone from getting too hot. Farther down the beach a game of volleyball was in progress. Elizabeth watched as a slender girl in cutoffs took a nose dive into the sand after a spiked ball.

"I thought you were never going to get here," Enid greeted as they plopped down beside her and George on the old chenille bedspread they were using as a beach blanket.

"Thanks for holding some space for us. Looks like you've been here quite a while," Elizabeth noted, as she took in the hot-pink color of Enid's formerly pale thighs. "If you don't put some suntan lotion on, you're going to look like a poached salmon pretty soon."

Enid sighed, rolling onto her stomach. "The price one pays for beauty. Can't you see I'm working on getting a tan?"

"More like getting crispy-fried," joked George, earning a dirty look from Enid over the rims of her sunglasses.

Todd stared out over the waves that rolled in offshore in nearly perfect four-foot green swells. He whistled in appreciation.

"Man, couldn't be better. Those waves are definitely made to order."

The judging hadn't started yet, but a number of wetsuited competitors bobbed beyond the swells, sometimes paddling in to take a wave as it curled into a crest. Elizabeth spotted Sonny Callahan down the beach, near the lifeguard station. The blond sun god didn't look the least bit worried as he straddled his board, waxing it with slow circular strokes while carrying on a conversation with an animated-looking Lila

Fowler. Lila, in her metallic-blue one-piece, her wavy light-brown hair done up in French braids, was practically draped over his board as she feigned a keen interest in surfing.

"Anyone seen Bill?" Elizabeth wanted to know.

"Not a hair of his hide," replied Enid, who was busy smoothing her legs with lotion.

"I think that's supposed to be 'neither hide nor hair,'" George corrected, slapping her shoulder playfully.

"Ouch! OK. No, I haven't seen Bill, come to think of it."

"No one has," George added.

"Do you think he'll show?" Sniffing a scoop in the works, Elizabeth dug into her oversize straw beach bag for the pad and pencil she always carried.

Enid shrugged. "Who knows? Bill's always been kind of a loner. He probably didn't tell anyone what he's up to."

"Maybe you were right, Enid." Elizabeth giggled. "Maybe he's really a double agent wanted by the FBI."

"The wet suit is only one of his many disguises, folks," George said in a stage-whisper. "Used mainly to smuggle secret information to enemy submarines."

The four of them giggled at the idea.

"He'd better turn up soon," Todd remarked. "They're going to start the contest any minute."

The judges occupied the lifeguard station, the highest vantage point on the beach. As Elizabeth shaded her eyes to look up, one of the judges, the owner of a local surf shop, raised a megaphone to his lips to announce that any competitor who didn't have a number by twelve o'clock would be disqualified.

Sonny Callahan strolled leisurely over to receive his number, then proceeded to suit up, bronze muscles rippling under Lila's adoring gaze.

George glanced at his watch. "Three minutes. Maybe he got kidnapped by a band of crazed pirates."

"Very likely," Enid scoffed. "One thing's for sure—if Bill doesn't show, he'll never live it down."

The crowd waited in suspense, heads craning for any sign of Bill Chase. Elizabeth had all but given up on him when a ripple of applause started up at the far end of the beach by the parking lot, working its way toward her as it grew to a deafening cheer. The sea of bodies parted, and she caught sight of Bill trotting toward the lifeguard station, a gleaming new surfboard tucked under one arm.

"Finally!" Todd breathed. "I was beginning to wonder if my board would ever have a crack at those waves."

"*Your* board?" Elizabeth piped.

Todd grinned at her. "My parents gave it to me on my last birthday, but I never got a chance to use it more than once or twice, so I sold it to Bill. He wanted an O'Neill, but he couldn't afford to buy a new one. That's how I got the rest of the money I needed for the Yamaha."

Elizabeth recalled seeing Todd and Bill huddled together in the corridor at school the week before, and it suddenly made sense. That was when Todd had told her he was getting the motorcycle.

"That still doesn't explain why he was missing for practically an entire week," said Enid.

"He swore me to secrecy—otherwise I would've told sooner. He cut school so he could practice on the new board."

"Look at him go!" George roared as Bill crouched into the first wave. He was just a hairbreadth behind Sonny.

To those watching from a distance, Bill seemed one with board and water, cutting a zigzag through the glassy curl as effortlessly as an ice skater doing figure eights. Sonny was good, too, but if Elizabeth had been a judge, she would have awarded more points to Bill for that wave.

Bill and Sonny remained neck and neck for the next couple of hours. There was no denying that Sonny was fast and clean, but in Elizabeth's opinion Bill had the better style.

He danced through the waves with a lightness and

balance that even Fred Astaire would have envied, she scribbled in her notebook.

Still, it was only her opinion. Some judges, she knew, favored power and speed over grace and style, so there was no way of guessing who had racked up more points.

She could hear Lila Fowler talking to someone behind her.

"No question about it. He makes Bill Chase look like a chimpanzee on skis. Did you see the way he cut in front of Bill just now? Oh, did I tell you he invited me out to a party afterwards? . . ."

A few of the other surfers with less experience had dropped out by the time the judges were getting ready to call the contest to a close. Dink Halstead limped up the beach after wiping out on some rocks. There was a thin trickle of blood on his cheek.

"I've had enough," he called to one of his friends. "Let David and Goliath battle it out. It's their show anyway."

Finally it was time for the judges to tabulate their points and announce the winner. Elizabeth held her breath as the voice over the megaphone blared the names of those in fourth and fifth places. Sonny and Bill were just now straggling in, looking exhausted as they peeled off their wet suits.

"In third place, with one hundred and eighty points, Gary Wallace. . . ."

A sprinkling of applause, and then the crowd held its breath.

"In second place, with two hundred and thirty points"—the megaphone squeaked, the shrill note scraping along Elizabeth's nerves like fingernails on a blackboard—"Sonny Callahan. And the champion with two hundred and thirty-six points—a close call, folks—is Bill Chase."

A wild cheer erupted. A number of Bill's fans surged down to lift him, enthroned atop his board, onto their shoulders. The normally low-keyed Bill raised a triumphant fist, grinning from ear to ear. Winston Egbert jammed a hastily woven crown of seaweed onto Bill's head. A dark-haired boy Elizabeth didn't recognize was busy pouring a can of beer over him as well. Bill snatched the can before it was empty and took a long swig, streams of foam dribbling down his face.

"You should call your article 'Rocky of the Deep,' " Enid suggested, contentedly munching on the hero sandwich she'd brought along.

"I've already got a title," said Elizabeth, holding up her note pad so they could see what she'd written: "Chase Is One."

"Clever," remarked Todd. "Very clever."

Sonny Callahan was engaged in a furious argument with the judges, a display of poor sportsmanship Elizabeth was quick to make note of. His golden aura of confidence had been tarnished. Even Lila seemed to have lost interest. She had joined the crowd that hovered about Bill, and she was congratulating him as if she'd known all along that he was going to win.

Cara spotted Elizabeth and her friends and rushed over.

"Where's Jessica?" she wanted to know. "I've been searching absolutely everywhere for her. Didn't she come with you?"

"Jessica couldn't make it," Elizabeth replied. "She's sick today."

"What's wrong with her?"

"Nothing too serious. Just a raging case of poison oak." Elizabeth didn't add that it was a result of getting lost in the woods the day Jessica had sneaked off with Scott.

"Gee, that's too bad," Cara remarked. "I know how much she was looking forward to this. Now she'll have to miss the party and everything. Is she really bummed out about it?"

"I'd say she wasn't too happy." Elizabeth suppressed a tiny smile, remembering Jessica's howls of rage when she discovered that the pesky little rash that had been plaguing her all week had erupted into a volcano of swollen, red blisters. Elizabeth was surprised at herself for not feeling sorrier for Jessica than she did, but she couldn't help wondering if Jessica didn't deserve it after all.

She recalled their mother's bewildered look as she shook her head over Jessica, wondering aloud, "I simply can't imagine where on earth you could have picked up such a thing. . . ."

Fourteen

"Had enough?" Todd draped an arm about Elizabeth's shoulder as they huddled near the crackling driftwood fire.

"If I eat one more marshmallow, I'm going to turn into one myself," she joked, snuggling against him as she licked the last of the sticky golden-brown sweet from her stick. An hour earlier she'd been hungry enough to devour two hot dogs, a generous helping of potato salad, and several root beers. It hardly seemed possible.

"I know what you mean," Todd said. "I can't remember the last time I ate so much. Unless you count Thanksgiving and Christmas."

When his lips found hers, she could taste the

smoky sweetness of toasted marshmallows. He kissed her lingeringly, drawing lazy circles against her back with the flat of his hand. Several other couples were cuddled under blankets by the fire, but Elizabeth felt uncomfortable about getting too affectionate in public. She drew away, tucking her head against his shoulder.

Reading her thoughts, Todd whispered, "Too bad we're not off somewhere by ourselves. I could get addicted to this."

"Me, too," she confessed.

"Let's go for a picnic next Saturday," he suggested. "Just the two of us. I know this great little cove where we can really be alone. It's private, but a friend of my aunt has a key to the gate."

"I'd love to go," Elizabeth said.

"Great. We'll take my motorcycle. I'm picking it up at the dealership on Friday. Wait until you see it, Liz! I'm even getting another helmet just for you."

Elizabeth stiffened. "Todd, I—"

"I know what you're thinking," he broke in, "but, listen, everyone's a little nervous the first time they ride on a motorcycle. Don't worry, you'll get used to it in no time."

"That's not it." She pulled away from him, tucking her knees against her chest. How could she tell him? She'd been postponing this moment, and now she couldn't put it off any longer.

114

"What is it, then?"

"I—"

They were interrupted just then by Ken Matthews and his date, petite, redheaded Julie Porter, who had sauntered over from the neighboring campfire to find a can opener.

"Some lamebrain lost ours in the sand," Ken explained. "He's over there now digging a hole to China trying to find it."

Elizabeth laughed. "Wish him luck for us. Hey, take the rest of these marshmallows while you're at it. I don't think I'll ever be able to look at another one as long as I live."

"Thanks!" Ken caught the bag she tossed in his direction as if he were intercepting a pass on the forty-yard line. "The same nerd who lost the can opener forgot to bring the marshmallows, too."

"Tell Winston we said hi," Todd deadpanned, earning a ripple of appreciative laughter from those who were familiar with Winston Egbert's clownish antics.

Someone had turned up a radio, and silky music riffled the warm night air. Snuggled under a blanket across from them, arms entwined, George and Enid held a quiet, intense conversation.

"I'm glad you decided not to go swimming with Jaws," Todd whispered, nuzzling Elizabeth's ear. He'd forgotten his earlier question

115

about the motorcycle, which left Elizabeth feeling relieved but also strangely depressed.

"I don't think it would have been nearly as much fun," she confided as she tipped her head back to receive his kiss. "Besides, I don't think sharks eat marshmallows, do they?"

Elizabeth pushed her nagging concern to the back of her mind, letting the sensation of Todd's kisses spread outward from her center like ripples on a pond. She knew she would have to tell him sooner or later. Her parents had forbidden, absolutely *forbidden*, either Jessica or herself to ride on a motorcycle. It was practically one of the Ten Commandments as far as they were concerned.

Elizabeth certainly understood why. A while back one of their cousins had been killed riding a motorcycle. She still remembered how upset their mom had been over it. If she knew Elizabeth was even *contemplating* getting on one of those things . . .

Elizabeth shuddered to think of the consequences.

And yet how would Todd take it when she refused to share what was obviously going to be a major part of his life from now on? It was sure to put a dent in their closeness, she realized with a sick feeling of dread.

"I'll bet you'd look cute in a crash helmet," Todd murmured as he twirled a lock of her hair about his finger. "Maybe I'll get you one in bright blue."

Elizabeth killed any further conversation on the subject by winding her arms about his neck and kissing him with such fervor that he fell backward onto the sand.

Tomorrow, she promised herself, stifling the tiny stitch of fear in the pit of her stomach. *I'll tell him tomorrow. . . .*

Will Todd's motorcycle drive them apart? Find out in Sweet Valley High #6, DANGEROUS LOVE.

Other books in the
Sweet Valley High
series you may have missed:

☐ **#1 DOUBLE LOVE** Meet the Wakefield twins, Elizabeth and Jessica. They're both popular, smart, and gorgeous, but that's where the similarity ends. Elizabeth is friendly, outgoing, and sincere—nothing like her twin. As snobbish and conniving as she is charming and vivacious, Jessica thinks the whole world revolves around her. Trouble is, most of the time it does. Jessica always gets what she wants—at school, with friends, and especially with boys. Even Elizabeth, who is usually wise to her twin sister's ways, has a hard time saying no to her.

This time Jessica has her sights set on Todd Wilkins, handsome star of the basketball team—

the one boy Elizabeth really likes. Todd likes Elizabeth, too, until Jessica starts interfering. There's nothing she won't do—from intercepting Todd's phone calls to wangling a date with Todd for the big dance. She even comes close to ruining her sister's reputation by letting the police think she's Elizabeth when she's picked up with troublemaker Rick Andover. Elizabeth is heartsick. She doesn't want to lose Todd, but it looks like he's falling for Jessica. Or is he?

□ #2 SECRETS Beautiful and ruthless, Jessica Wakefield is determined to be chosen queen of the fall dance at Sweet Valley High. If she can win the contest, she's sure to win Bruce Patman, the most sought-after boy in school.

The only person standing in Jessica's way is Enid Rollins. When Jessica discovers the truth about Enid's past—a secret so shameful Enid is terrified at the thought of anyone finding out— she knows the crown is within her grasp. She doesn't care that Enid is her twin sister Elizabeth's best friend—or that revealing the secret may cost Enid both her reputation and the boy she loves.

When Jessica lets the cat out of the bag— anonymously, of course—Enid is doubly stricken. Elizabeth was the only one who knew, she thinks; it must have been Elizabeth who betrayed her! Can Elizabeth convince Enid it wasn't her fault? Or will her scheming twin once again get away with murder?

☐ **#3 PLAYING WITH FIRE** Watch out, Sweet Valley High! Jessica Wakefield is at it again. This time Jessica proceeds to sink her hooks into rich, handsome Bruce Patman, the most sophisticated guy at Sweet Valley High.

Or is it the other way around—has Bruce gotten his hooks into Jessica? Elizabeth notices a big change in her sister. In the past, Jessica had only to give a boy one of her dazzling smiles, and he would come running. Now suddenly she's following Bruce everywhere and dropping everything, including cheerleading, just to spend time with him.

Elizabeth doesn't trust Bruce one bit—he's arrogant, demanding, and way too fast. Jessica can usually hold her own with any guy, but this time Elizabeth's afraid her sister may be going too far.

☐ **#4 POWER PLAY** Chubby Robin Wilson has been following Jessica around for months. First she wanted to be her friend—now she wants to join Pi Beta Alpha, Sweet Valley High's snobby sorority.

When Elizabeth, Jessica's twin, nominates Robin for the sorority, Jessica is furious. Robin may be friendly and smart, but she's certainly not beautiful or popular enough to be a Pi Beta. Worst of all, she's fat. Jessica and her snobby friends are determined to find a way to keep Robin out.

But Elizabeth is just as determined to make Robin a sorority sister. Soon the twins are locked in a struggle that develops into the biggest power play at Sweet Valley High. But Robin has the biggest surprise of all in store for her enemies.

A special bonus for fans of Sweet Valley High! Here's more about some of the people you've met in Sweet Valley and would like to know better. . . .

☐ **BILL CHASE** The kind of guy people at Sweet Valley High love to speculate about. He's good-looking—a real California golden boy with wind-tossed blond hair, summer-blue eyes, and a deep tan—but he's somewhat of a loner. He hangs out at the beach a lot and seems to answer only to the call of the waves. Bill practically lives to surf, and he's really good, too. He's already won several surfing championships and plans to go to the world championship in Hawaii someday.

Girls, especially Jessica Wakefield, are attracted to him, but he seems immune to their flirtations.

Once, Jessica really went after Bill, even going so far as to ask him to a dance. He turned her down, and she was furious. Nobody had ever turned her down before! She's been looking for a way to get back at him ever since. Knowing Jessica, she'll find it, too.

What most people don't know about Bill is that he's terribly shy. One of the reasons he likes surfing so much is because it's a solitary sport. He feels most content when he's alone out on the water, at one with the wind, the waves, and the sky. No wonder his favorite book is Hemingway's *The Old Man and the Sea*. Bill feels very close to the ocean, and though he hasn't discussed this with anyone yet, he's thinking about becoming a marine biologist someday. In spite of the time he puts in at the beach, he's a pretty good student. His grades are high enough to get him into college after he graduates.

Another thing people don't know about Bill is that he had a girlfriend once, someone he loved deeply. It was before his parents got divorced and he moved with his mother from Santa Monica to Sweet Valley. Her name was Julianne. They went steady for two years and had even talked about getting married someday. They were devoted to each other and enjoyed doing all the same things together. Julianne was a surf nut like Bill. One of the things they loved best was getting up at the crack of dawn, piling into Bill's truck with their surfboards, and driving down to the beach. They would watch the sunrise while they rode the waves. Bill can never forget how wonderful it was sharing his life with Julianne.

It ended two days before her sixteenth birthday, when she was killed in a horrible car accident. Bill, haunted by her death, blamed himself. They'd had an argument that night. They were at a party, so she grabbed a ride home with someone else—a boy who had been drinking. It was raining, and his car skidded out of control and hit an embankment. Julianne died instantly.

If only they hadn't gotten into that silly argument! he thought over and over. If only he'd insisted on driving her home himself!

For a long time he couldn't even look at another girl without seeing Julianne's face. The night after she died, he went surfing even though there was a storm raging. He nearly drowned. The result was a bad case of pneumonia that kept him in bed for weeks. During that time, he thought a lot about Julianne and finally came to the conclusion that she wouldn't want him to blame himself for her death. She was much too sweet and generous for that. He realized that the right way for him to remember their love was to go on living as best he could.

It's been almost a year, and there have been a lot of changes in his life since then. He's had to adjust to his parents' divorce. Bill was really close to his father, from whom he inherited his freewheeling spirit and love of the outdoors. Bill's father is a forest ranger who lives in Idaho now. The previous winter, Bill spent Christmas in the mountains with his father and discovered he liked skiing almost as much as surfing.

Bill has more trouble getting along with his mother. She's the nervous type and is always afraid Bill is going to hurt himself. They argue a lot about his surfing, which she thinks is dangerous. Bill loves her, but he's not going to let her run his life the way he thinks she tried to run his father's. In his own quiet way, he's very strong-willed.

All in all, Bill is getting his life together again. He'll never forget Julianne, but he doesn't ache so much for her anymore. He would even like to fall in love again, but he doesn't feel ready to make a move with any of the girls he knows. The only girl he can really talk to is Elizabeth Wakefield, and she already has a boyfriend. Sometimes, when he's depressed, he's afraid he'll never find someone to love the way he loved Julianne.

Little does Bill know what fate has in store for him where love is concerned!

126

☐ **LILA FOWLER** Pretty, rich, spoiled, and the daughter of George Fowler, one of the richest men in Sweet Valley. The Fowlers represent the new money brought into the valley by the prospering computer-chip industry. They're in direct opposition to the Patmans, once the most powerful family in town, who are fighting to keep Sweet Valley the same as it was thirty years ago, when the big industry was canning.

Lila's main concern in life is status and image. She's one of the biggest snobs at Sweet Valley High. She has little patience for those who don't measure up to her standards. It's one of the reasons she and Jessica are such good friends. Together they intend to keep Pi Beta Alpha, the snobby sorority to which they belong, free of nerds, fatties, and other types they've deemed undesirable. Elizabeth steers clear of Lila whenever possible. If there's one thing she hates, it's snobs.

The truth about Lila, though, is that she's very insecure. Although she has a sleek, sophisticated image, she feels unloved and neglected. Her parents have always given her anything she wanted—except their attention. Now they're divorced, and she's living with her father, who travels a lot of the time. Mother is living it up in Europe with her jet-setter friends. Lila is an only child, so she doesn't have any brothers or sisters to hang out with. A live-in housekeeper is her closest companion at home. Though Lila would never admit it to anyone, she's so lonely she could scream.

Once Lila was caught shoplifting in the mall. Her father couldn't understand it. Why would she steal something she could easily afford to buy? If she needed more money, why didn't she just ask him? He doesn't realize that Lila was trying to get his attention the only way she could. Obviously, being pretty, popular, and talented isn't enough.

Something she found out this year has made her more insecure than ever. During one of her mother's infrequent visits, she admitted to Lila that George Fowler isn't her real father. Mrs. Fowler was pregnant with Lila when she met him, but he agreed to marry her and give the baby his name. Lila sees him in a new, more unselfish light, but at the same time she's worried sick. Since she's not George's real daughter, maybe he'll lose interest in her altogether someday. Maybe that's the reason he doesn't want to spend time with her, she thinks. She's terrified he'll get married again and have a child of his own. Also, she wonders about her real father. Who is he? Her mother won't tell. "Better not to open old wounds," she tells Lila. Nevertheless, Lila is dying of curiosity. Maybe he's someone rich and famous—a Hollywood celebrity. Her mother used to be a bit actress in Hollywood before she met George. Now, whenever Lila goes to the movies with her friends, she searches the faces of the actors on screen for any resemblance of her.

When Lila's mind isn't on her father, she's thinking about boys. The summer before, while visiting relatives in Boston, she fell in love with a boy named Ted Whitlock. For once in her life, Lila learned what it was like to be looked down upon. The Whitlocks are old, old Boston society—their ancestors came over on the *Mayflower*. Ted was crazy about Lila, but his parents didn't approve. Lila wasn't socially acceptable as far as they were concerned. Nevertheless, Lila and Ted managed to sneak out together quite a bit. They played tennis, went for long walks, and hid out in museums and movie theaters. When it was time for Lila to return home, they kissed tearfully and promised to write. Well, Lila wrote—five letters. Ted wrote her once—to ask her why she hadn't written. Lila's positive his parents have been intercepting the letters she sent him. The one time she tried to phone, Mrs. Whitlock icily informed her Ted wasn't home. Lila is desperate for some way to show Ted she still cares. He's the most fantastic guy she's ever met—also the richest and most well-connected. The boys she's dated at Sweet Valley High are nothing compared to Ted.

Lila's dream is to marry Ted Whitlock someday. Also, she wants to become a professional tennis star like her idol, Chris Evert Lloyd. When she's a big star, married to a man who's even richer than her father, then Daddy will have to notice her, won't he?

COMING ATTRACTIONS

Scenes from the next episode of Sweet Valley High, *DANGEROUS LOVE*

"Todd sure doesn't waste any time, does he?" Jessica said. Her contempt for Todd was thick enough to cut with a knife.

Elizabeth almost dropped the dish she was rinsing. "I don't know what you're talking about," she declared, staring down at the dinner plate as if it were the most important thing on earth.

"Come on, Liz, we all saw Mandy get off that bike with Todd. You know what I mean."

"I'm not sure I do."

"Well, it's obvious that Todd feels the need to keep the backseat of his bike warm."

Elizabeth finished rinsing the plate, then

handed it to her sister. "Oh, Jess, you're just jumping to conclusions. Give me a break, OK?"

But Jessica was undeterred. "Listen, Elizabeth," Jessica continued, putting the plate into the dishwasher, "didn't you notice the way Mandy was holding on to Todd as they pulled up? It didn't look so innocent to me."

"How else was she supposed to stay on the bike?" Elizabeth snapped back as she handed Jessica another plate. But even though Todd had explained it to her, she was still upset. And she didn't like feeling that way at all. "It was no big deal," she added, echoing Todd's earlier words. "She and Todd are working on a class project together. So he gave her a lift. He was just being friendly."

"*You* may see it that way, but *I* don't. A guy who's 'just being friendly,' wouldn't let a girl drape herself all over him like that, and you know it. In case you haven't noticed, those bikes have arm rails on them."

"I didn't know you knew so much about motorcycles."

"Let's just say that I know enough about them to know I wouldn't tolerate *my* boyfriend riding one."

"You're making too much out of this," Elizabeth said. "Anyway, Todd's coming over tonight to talk to Mom and Dad. He wants to try to convince them to change their rule about no motorcycle rides."

Jessica close the dishwasher door with a thud. "You don't mean to tell me you're actually thinking about getting on that motorcycle?"

"Well, no . . ." Elizabeth wavered. "But

Todd insists it's safe. And lots of people ride around without getting hurt."

"And a lot of others get killed—like Rexy!" Jessica shouted angrily.

"Jess, please calm down—"

"I'm not sticking around to listen to you talk about that death machine. If anyone wants me, I'll be at Cara's!" Jessica turned on her heel and stormed out of the room.

"Todd, tell me now!" Elizabeth demanded. "What have you been doing all night?"

Todd grew serious. "I've made a decision about us. And the bike." He patted the bike's gas tank, which gleamed in the moonlight. "It's the most difficult decision I've ever had to make, but it's something I have to do."

Elizabeth felt sick. Her anger at Todd dissipated as a sobering, dark thought set in. Todd's missing the party had nothing to do with his grandfather or with traffic. The "things" he'd had to take care of definitely had something to do with her. He sounded so solemn, she had the awful feeling she'd drawn the short straw in his choice between her and the motorcycle.

This wasn't the way it was supposed to be. Didn't the tender kisses they'd shared and the promises of love they'd exchanged mean anything to him? "Go on, Todd, get it over with," she said glumly.

"I know you may not understand this—"

"Just say it, Todd, will you?" she pleaded, her eyes brimming with tears.

*   *   *

Jessica and Brian left Miller's Point and headed down the hill on the main road leading to town. About halfway there they noticed that, up ahead, the darkened roadway was illuminated with the eerie red glow of traffic flares. Moving closer, they spotted the flashing red bubble lights of two Sweet Valley police cars.

"Looks like an accident," Brian said as he eased off the gas pedal.

"Must be a bad one, too. I think I hear an ambulance coming," Jessica noted.

Brian slowed to a crawl as they neared the accident site. "Look," he said, pointing to a purple van parked on the opposite side of the road. "Doesn't look damaged at all. Probably just a breakdown."

Jessica was just about to nod in agreement when she spotted the broken remains of a black motorcycle lying about a hundred feet beyond the van. "Oh my God!" she cried out when the awful realization sank in. "I think that's Todd's bike. Brian, we've got to stop!"

Jessica slumped in her seat as Brian eased off the road and parked. It looked bad. Todd was probably hurt. Or maybe even dead, she realized with a shudder. How was she going to tell Elizabeth?